MW01156272

Longarm reined away from the Mexican side, turned in the saddle, and threw two more shots as suppressing fire.

Only one rifle answered as Longarm headed back toward U.S. soil.

He turned the other way and tried to take aim at that shooter, but suddenly the brown lost its footing and went down in the middle of the Rio Grande.

The horse threw its head and coughed, then rolled onto its side and went under.

Icy cold water closed over Longarm's head.

He tried to kick free of the saddle but his spur was hung up in the stirrup.

The horse kicked and thrashed in its death throes, keeping Longarm from reaching down to his boot.

He had not had time to take a breath before going under the water. He opened his mouth reflexively and muddy water rushed in. He had only seconds left to live . . .

DON'T MISS THESE
ALL-ACTION WESTERN SERIES
FROM THE BERKLEY PUBLISHING GROUP

THE GUNSMITH by J. R. Roberts

Clint Adams was a legend among lawmen, outlaws, and ladies. They called him . . . the Gunsmith.

LONGARM by Tabor Evans

The popular long-running series about Deputy U.S. Marshal Custis Long—his life, his loves, his fight for justice.

SLOCUM by Jake Logan

Today's longest-running action Western. John Slocum rides a deadly trail of hot blood and cold steel.

BUSHWHACKERS by B. J. Lanagan

An action-packed series by the creators of Longarm! The rousing adventures of the most brutal gang of cutthroats ever assembled—Quantrill's Raiders.

DIAMONDBACK by Guy Brewer

Dex Yancey is Diamondback, a Southern gentleman turned con man when his brother cheats him out of the family fortune. Ladies love him. Gamblers hate him. But nobody pulls one over on Dex . . .

WILDGUN by Jack Hanson

The blazing adventures of mountain man Will Barlow—from the creators of Longarm!

TEXAS TRACKER by Tom Calhoun

J.T. Law: the most relentless—and dangerous—manhunter in all Texas. Where sheriffs and posses fail, he's the best man to bring in the most vicious outlaws—for a price.

TABOR EVANS

LONGARM

AND THE
ONE-ARMED BANDIT

JOVE BOOKS, NEW YORK

THE BERKLEY PUBLISHING GROUP
Published by the Penguin Group
Penguin Group (USA) Inc.
375 Hudson Street, New York, New York 10014, USA
Penguin Group (Canada), 90 Eglinton Avenue East, Suite 700, Toronto, Ontario M4P 2Y3, Canada
(a division of Pearson Penguin Canada Inc.)
Penguin Books Ltd., 80 Strand, London WC2R 0RL, England
Penguin Group Ireland, 25 St. Stephen's Green, Dublin 2, Ireland (a division of Penguin Books Ltd.)
Penguin Group (Australia), 250 Camberwell Road, Camberwell, Victoria 3124, Australia
(a division of Pearson Australia Group Pty. Ltd.)
Penguin Books India Pvt. Ltd., 11 Community Centre, Panchsheel Park, New Delhi—110 017, India
Penguin Group (NZ), 67 Apollo Drive, Rosedale, North Shore 0632, New Zealand
(a division of Pearson New Zealand Ltd.)
Penguin Books (South Africa) (Pty.) Ltd., 24 Sturdee Avenue, Rosebank, Johannesburg 2196,
South Africa

Penguin Books Ltd., Registered Offices: 80 Strand, London WC2R 0RL, England

This is a work of fiction. Names, characters, places, and incidents either are the product of the author's imagination or are used fictitiously, and any resemblance to actual persons, living or dead, business establishments, events, or locales is entirely coincidental.

LONGARM AND THE ONE-ARMED BANDIT

A Jove Book / published by arrangement with the author

PRINTING HISTORY
Jove edition / July 2010

Copyright © 2010 by Penguin Group (USA) Inc.
Cover illustration by Miro Sinovcic.

All rights reserved.
No part of this book may be reproduced, scanned, or distributed in any printed or electronic form without permission. Please do not participate in or encourage piracy of copyrighted materials in violation of the author's rights. Purchase only authorized editions.
For information, address: The Berkley Publishing Group,
a division of Penguin Group (USA) Inc.,
375 Hudson Street, New York, New York 10014.

ISBN: 978-0-515-14815-2

JOVE®
Jove Books are published by The Berkley Publishing Group,
a division of Penguin Group (USA) Inc.,
375 Hudson Street, New York, New York 10014.
JOVE® is a registered trademark of Penguin Group (USA) Inc.
The "J" design is a trademark of Penguin Group (USA) Inc.

PRINTED IN THE UNITED STATES OF AMERICA

10 9 8 7 6 5 4 3 2 1

If you purchased this book without a cover, you should be aware that this book is stolen property. It was reported as "unsold and destroyed" to the publisher, and neither the author nor the publisher has received any payment for this "stripped book."

Chapter 1

Custis Long yawned. Snorted. Struggled to open an eye glued closed by last night's dissipation, succeeded with one eye and then the other. It took him a moment to remember where he was, and when he did he kept his eyes on the ceiling rather than glance toward the person snoring beside him.

He felt a crawling, itching sensation down beside his balls, reached down, and pushed his limp, sticky dick aside so he could reach the spot and scratch. Lordy, he hoped his companion hadn't shared a crop of crabs with him. Or worse.

"Mmm, hey there, darlin'. G'morning." Her voice was whiskey rough. "You want a little eye-opener, sweetie? You wanta fuck?" Her fingers sought him out, and despite his misgivings about the woman his damned cock betrayed him . . . it started to rise and shine. Well, rise anyway.

Deputy United States Marshal Long was not yet up to speaking. Instead he reached over and gave the back of her head a push, shoving her face toward his dick. She got the message, bent down, and began to suck. It was, he figured, as good a way as any to clean last night's used cum off. And better than most.

The woman—he could not begin to recall her name—was making wet, gobbling noises and kept scraping him with her teeth. He decided to forgive her. She could really suck. He placed the flat of his hand between her shoulder blades by way of encouragement and began to thrust into her mouth harder and deeper until with a grunt of effort he shot a wad of cum into her throat.

She giggled and sat upright, and he got a good look at her. There must have been some reason why he chose her, he thought, but damned if he could think of it now. For sure it was not because of her beauty.

"Gu . . . argh." He coughed, cleared his throat, and tried again. "Good morning, pretty girl." She was years past being a girl, but what the hell. "Pour some water in that basin an' wash me off, will ya?"

She jumped to obey. She had big tits, he saw, but they were sloppy big, the flesh wrinkled and suety. There was nothing pretty about them. Nor about the rest of her, either, for that matter. In the harsh light of morning she was just an aging, used-up whore.

He smiled at her. "Thanks."

The woman—what in hell *was* her name, anyway—reacted like a puppy given a pat when it was expecting a kick. She smiled back at him, laid the washcloth aside, and leaned down to plant a light kiss on the tip of his dick. Like any good whore she knew not to kiss him on the mouth, but a peck on the pecker came from the heart. Longarm caressed her cheek and gently kissed her forehead. The woman beamed at the compliment.

"Nathan," she said shyly, "could I ask you something, honey?"

"O' course," he told her.

"You said your name is Nathan James, right?"

"Uh-huh, that's right."

"Are you . . . do you happen to be kin to Jesse James, Nathan honey?"

Longarm chuckled. "I kind of wish I was. An' for all I know maybe I am, but what I know for sure is that I'm not close kin to Frank and Jesse. They're from Missouri. My people are from West Virginia."

"I hope you don't mind me asking, because, well, you know," she said in a voice that was little more than a whisper.

"No offense taken," he assured her.

"I swear, Nathan, you're just the nicest man there ever was. Any time you want me, darlin', all you have to do is to crook your finger and I'll come running."

"I'll sure do it, too. Now move, please. I need t' get up an' I don't want t' kick you when I sit up."

The woman quickly stood and jumped out of the way so Longarm could sit up and swing his long legs off the side of the sagging bed. "Is there anything I can do for you, honey?" she asked. "Would you like me to give you a shave? I'm good at that, and it would pleasure me to tend to you a bit, you being such a fine gentleman and all."

"That would be all right. Sure," he said.

"Then you just wait right here, Nathan. I'll get some hot water and a good razor and cake of soap and whatnot. I'll be right back, quick as I can."

"That sounds fine."

She grabbed a red-and-blue kimono off a hook on the wall and took off in a rush. Longarm lighted a cheroot and smoked it until she got back.

"I told you I wouldn't be long."

"So you did," he agreed, "an' you was true to your word."

She patted hot water onto his face, then wrapped his head in a warm towel while she whipped the soap into a lather, removed the towel, and brushed the lather on. She did not have a strop with her so he hoped the razor was already good and sharp or he was apt to have a bad experience here.

As it turned out the woman really did know what she was doing with a razor. She had a light, feathery touch.

Longarm leaned back, closed his eyes, and pondered the events of the past few days that had brought him to this room, under a false name and without the privileges—and the protections—conveyed by a lawman's badge.

The woman hummed as she worked on him, a smile on her face.

Chapter 2

A cold day in Denver it had been, not at all like the border warmth down in Texas. The crispness of Denver's cold was invigorating though. Constant heat just seemed to make a man sleepy. It had been cold that last time he walked down Colfax to the Federal Building, across the street from the U.S. Mint, and up the steps to the long familiar corridor that led to U.S. Marshal William Vail's office.

Billy Vail's clerk Henry was in his usual position bent over his desk, working on some form or other. Lordy, there were more than enough forms to be filled out for every little thing. Longarm could not begin to keep track of them all. Lucky for the whole office that Henry could.

Longarm walked in, a tall man, well over six feet in height, with broad shoulders and narrow hips. He had seal brown hair and a handlebar mustache. His face was deeply tanned from years spent in the saddle. Deputy Long did not consider himself to be particularly handsome . . . but a good many ladies found him so. His eyes were a warm brown, almost golden in color, but they could turn as hard as slate if he was crossed.

He customarily wore a snuff-brown, low-crowned Stetson hat and black, knee-high cavalry boots with flat walk-

ing heels and—when needed—plain spurs with no rowels
that might make noise at times when silence was called for.
He carried a double-action Colt revolver in .45 caliber, worn
in a black leather cross-draw rig set just to the left of his
belt buckle.

On this particular morning Longarm tossed his Stetson
onto one of the curved arms on a coat rack near the entrance to Marshal Vail's private office and greeted the marshal's slender, bookish clerk. "Mornin' there, Henry. Is the
boss in?"

"Why do you ask?"

"Because I am sick an' damn tired of serving papers an'
transporting prisoners from jail cells to courtrooms. I wanta
get out an' stretch my legs some."

"You could always take a long walk, Longarm. And I do
mean long," Henry returned.

"I would, but I'd better not. Somethin' might come up
an' the boss might need me. Whatever would he do without
me?"

"Your incredible modesty is one of the things I most admire about you, Longarm."

"Yeah, it is pretty impressive, idn' it?" Longarm said with
a grin.

"To answer your question, yes," Henry said.

"Which question was that?"

"Yours."

"Damnit, Henry!"

The clerk chuckled, took a slim stack of papers from a
box on his desk and glanced at them, then said, "Your question, as I recall, was whether the marshal is in. Fact of the
matter is, he is not. He and all the other United States mar-
shals in the country have been called to Washington for a
conference. The attorney general has been asked by Congress to gather information. This conference is part of the
process."

"All right," Longarm said. "Am I s'posed t' be impressed?"

"Impressed? Perhaps not. But I think you will be interested," Henry said, holding up one of the papers he had just retrieved.

"An' what would that part be?"

"This is the part that involves you, Longarm."

Longarm's interest quickened. "Go on. Don't leave me hangin' here."

"As you know . . . or possibly don't if you haven't been reading the newspapers lately, Congress is considering passing new laws restricting the immigration of Chinese into this country. We already have protocols in place with the government of China that are supposed to limit the flow of Chinese here, but those don't seem to be working very well. Despite our laws the Chinese just continue to come. And our government does not know how they are doing this. We keep watch on the Pacific coast ports, but that has little effect.

"What they are asking you to do, Custis, you and a number of other agents of the United States, is to look into this problem. How are the Chinese illegals getting into the country. And where. We already know 'why,' of course. They come here for economic opportunity that they don't have at home. And they come. And they come. And still come in. Somehow. Billy Vail wants you to go down to the border and see if you could learn anything there about Chinese immigrants coming into the country illegally."

"It's a long border," Longarm said.

"You aren't being asked to personally walk every inch of it," Henry said. "Just go down there. See if you can learn anything about how those people are managing to circumvent our immigration agreements with China."

"All right," Longarm said.

"There is one more thing," Henry said.

"Just one?"

"One more should be enough. Billy suggested . . . he did say it is a suggestion, not an order . . . he suggested you do it without making it known that you are his deputy. Or anybody's, actually."

Longarm raised an eyebrow. "What the hell is that about?"

"The secretary of the interior has already sent two people down to see what they could learn. The two were open about their mission. They announced themselves. Hired a wagon and drove down along the border. They have not been heard from since. The wagon was found. Empty. Its mules still in harness. There was no sign of the secretary's investigators. There still has not been."

"So Billy wants me t' go down there with a closed mouth an' wide-open ears," Longarm said.

"In a word . . . yes." Henry nodded and sat back in his chair. It was not yet eight thirty in the morning, but he already looked tired, his eyes serious behind the glass windowpanes of his spectacles.

"You say I can't use my badge?"

"That's right. I know what you are thinking. That means you can't use it or expense vouchers for travel and meals and the like. You will have to pay with cash. I can arrange for you to have a line of credit that will be accepted at most banks on this side of the border. For anything else"—Henry shrugged—"you'll just have to work it out."

Actually Longarm had not given thought to money matters. He was just musing aloud when he made the comment, but he was glad Henry anticipated the need and took care of it for him.

"To begin with," Henry said, "I will write out an authorization for you to draw a thousand dollars or so. Do you have a money belt?"

Longarm shook his head.

"Get one. A traveling man would be expected to have a money belt."

"Is there any particular approach Billy wants me t' take? Anything he wants me t' be?"

"No. You are free to handle this however you like. The area where he wants you to work is within fifty miles or so, either direction, from the crossing at El Paso. Downstream from there and further west there will be others, some deputies and some not, some possibly working undercover. Or not. All you are responsible for is that El Paso corridor."

"All right. Is there a time limit here?"

"Not really. God knows when Congress in its great wisdom will get around to doing anything, possibly not for a year or more. Our job is just to give them information. What they do with it, if anything, will be up to them. May I suggest that you use a false name down there?"

"Why is that, Henry?"

"Your own name is fairly well known, especially among the criminal element. If illegals are being smuggled across the border, it is only logical to assume that criminals are the ones doing it. Well, by definition they are. I'm just thinking about the possibility that professional criminals may be involved, and if so someone might well recognize your name. Pick something else. Your choice. I'll arrange your line of credit in that name. And, come to think of it, I'd best establish an address here so we can communicate. I can assign myself a false company name so you can send telegrams there." He paused for a moment to think, then continued, "There is a telegraph office on Tremont. It isn't so very far. I can stop by there every day on my lunch break to collect any messages you might send."

"Henry, you don't take lunch breaks. You almost always eat here in the office," Longarm reminded the little man.

"I will take them faithfully while you are away. Now go home. Pack your things. This trip will be a little different since you'll not have your badge, so you probably shouldn't take your normal travel bag. Think about a name that . . ."

"Nathan James," Longarm blurted without taking time for serious thought.

"Good name," Henry said. "I like it. Wherever did that come from? You haven't used it before, have you?"

"Nope. Never thought of it before," Longarm admitted. "Damned if I'd know where it come from." In truth he did know. Earlier that morning he had overheard a veteran of the War between the States bragging—perhaps truthfully or perhaps not—about serving with Nathan Bedford Forrest. And standing in front of Henry's desk he could see a poster board over Henry's shoulder that was papered with Wanted posters including one for Jesse James. The two seemed to fit together nicely into Nathan James as an alias.

"Good. Write down the spelling that you want, and I'll make the arrangements. I should have everything done by the time you get back this afternoon."

Longarm left the office and headed for the rented room that was as close as he came to having a home. While he walked he thought about where he could hide his badge that would be absolutely secure. But within reach.

Sure, he was told he should not carry it with him on this trip.

But Billy Vail and Henry were not the ones who would be naked out there. If worse came to worst, Longarm wanted to be able to fall back on his badge. Did not want anyone to find it though if things went to shit.

He thought about the question for about four blocks. Then he turned on his heels and headed back the way he had just come, heading for a shoemaker's shop where he had done business in the past.

Chapter 3

In a seedy little pawn shop on Sixteenth, cluttered with dusty crap of all kinds—including a good many items that Longarm could not for the life of him figure out what they were meant for—he found a battered but basically sound Gladstone bag to temporarily replace his usual carpetbag. Not that there was anything wrong with the carpetbag, but they had very negative connotations among some people, and this time out Longarm was expected to blend into the woodwork, not piss anyone off.

Just observe and report back, Henry said. The idiots in Washington wanted to know things and it was up to him to tell them.

He took the Gladstone back to the shoemaker's he left earlier in the day. He needed to have the helpful fellow replace a broken hinge on the bag . . . and to pick up his holster.

"Damn good job there, Anton," he said, turning the holster over and over, examining it from all sides.

"Thank you," the shoemaker said with a little bow and a bob of his head. The man had white hair and a slight build. He spoke with an accent and came from some country that

Longarm was not sure he could find on a map, but the man did good work.

"I' tell you the truth, Anton, I can't see anyplace where you replaced the stitching."

Anton's smile spread even wider.

"It's really in there? For sure?"

"Oh, yes. Really is so. If you want it out, sir, you cut these stitches here. Peel the leather back and there it will be. One thing I should tell you. You wear this thing so very long, the little piece you have me sew inside will start to show. Just the outline, but the leather will mold to it."

Longarm's brow creased with worry. "Really? How long before that might could happen, Anton?"

The shoemaker shrugged. "Two, three years. Depends on how much you wear it."

Longarm relaxed. There was no damn way he would be working on this Chinese immigrant thing that long. The gentleman known as Nathan James would disappear long before then.

"Can you fix this while I wait here?" Longarm asked, lifting the Gladstone onto the counter.

While Anton looked at the hinge, Longarm very grate-fully threaded his holster—with his deputy marshal's badge hidden inside—back onto its belt, took the .45 out of his coat pocket, and returned the Colt to its proper place in the holster. The rig was a little thicker now, but a few tries assured him that the Colt came out of the leather just as smoothly as before. He felt better—more complete somehow—once the .45 was back at his waist where it belonged.

"Well?" he asked when he saw Anton set the Gladstone aside.

"You give me twenty minutes, then pick up, okay?"

"That sounds like a deal. Twenty minutes. I'll be back."

He went outside and walked down the street to a tobac-conist's shop. Damn but it smelled good in there. Different from the scents of leather in Anton's, but every bit as good.

Longarm took his time admiring the available stock in the tobacconist's, bought a box of Hernandez y Hernandez, and ambled back to Anton's shop. The Gladstone was waiting for him.

"How much do I owe you?" he asked.

Anton shrugged. "This, it was nothing. Just the hinge. Say . . . fifty cents."

"And the holster?"

"For that, since I know who you are and what you do, my friend, that little bit of sewing is my pleasure to give. No charge."

"That ain't right, Anton. I can pay, y'know."

"Yes. Please. Fifty cents."

Longarm gave the man a dollar and strode out, Gladstone in hand. He needed to rustle up some lunch, then go back to his boardinghouse and pack for the trip south.

He stifled a yawn while he walked. This Chinese thing was likely to be boring, he expected. But El Paso was a pleasant town. Lots of senoritas there with raven hair and flashing eyes. Could be this assignment would not be *completely* boring.

Chapter 4

The D&RG coach out of Denver was crowded as far south as Colorado Springs and Manitou Springs, thinned out a little down to Pueblo, and then was almost empty for the run to the terminus at El Moro. There was no club car attached after a stop in Pueblo so Longarm no longer had the amusement of a card game and a cigar to pass the time. Instead he settled onto one of the cleaner seats of the many that were available, crossed his legs, yawned, and closed his eyes. He drifted off into a light sleep within moments.

"Sir? Sir. I'm sorry to disturb you, sir, but would you mind giving me room so I can have that seat?"

He opened his eyes to a perfect vision of loveliness. Well, almost perfect. Perfect would have involved her being naked. Which she was not, damnit. But she was undeniably lovely.

The girl standing over him was young. Early twenties, he guessed. With the perfect skin of youth, light brown curls escaping beneath her bonnet. Clear, lovely, bright blue eyes. Apple cheeks and Cupid's bow lips. Long, dark eyelashes modestly lowered. Slender but with the details of her figure hidden beneath a light green traveling gown. Carrying an awkwardly large hatbox in a color matching her gown.

"If you are quite done examining me, sir . . . ?"

"Oh. Right. Sorry." Longarm uncrossed his legs, giving the girl room to move past him onto the seat facing his.

She took her time getting settled onto the thinly padded railcar seat. The hatbox she set directly opposite Longarm while she was beside the window out of which he could see the distant Culebra Range and the detent where La Veta Pass would be. He seemed to have slept away most of the trip below Pueblo.

"And where are you bound, sir?"

"South. El Paso. D'you know it?"

"El Paso? No, I've never been there. The truth is that I've never been anywhere."

"Really?"

"Almost. I went to visit my aunt in Canon City once. That was exciting. I was frightened, all those murderers and robbers and whatnot behind the walls of that big old prison there. Have you seen it? It is awful. Simply awful."

"Yes, I've seen it, all right. It scares me, too."

"I should be more adventuresome, I suppose, but I couldn't help being frightened."

"Of course you couldn't," Longarm agreed.

She peered out the window at the scenery rolling past the coach windows. "I wonder if people can look inside."

"Inside these windows?"

"Inside that prison."

"I don't think so. Even if you committed a crime you wouldn't be sent there. Ladies have their own prison over in Florence."

"Really? Ooo!" She shuddered and hugged her arms to herself. "How awful. Do ladies really go to prison?"

"If they commit crimes, they do. You might be surprised how many women do. They poison their husbands or steal from their neighbors or do all manner of things that put them behind bars when they are caught." He smiled. "But I don't suppose you should call them ladies as they most surely are not."

"Do you think I am a lady?"

"You look the part. Remains t' be seen if you act like a lady."

"And if I am not?"

Longarm's smile turned into a grin that wrinkled the corners of his eyes. "Then I reckon I'd talk t' you a little different."

The girl laughed. "I like you, sir. You aren't at all like the rough-talking coal miners who work for my daddy. You, sir, are a gentleman."

"Just shows how looks can deceive, don't it."

"Would it be forward of me to inquire about your name, sir?"

"I wouldn't mind that at all." He came very near to spitting out his real name from sheer habit, forgetting for the moment what he was doing here. And who he was for the time being. "Nathan James, miss."

"And I am Amanda Sue Crocker, Mr. James. I'm pleased to meet you." She leaned forward and held out a small, silk-gloved hand for him to gently shake in greeting.

"My pleasure, Miss Crocker."

"Amanda," she corrected.

"And I'm Nathan."

The girl giggled, fluffed her travel gown out wide, then impulsively switched seats, coming forward to wedge herself in between Longarm and the coach windows. She linked her hand through his arm and lay her pretty head on his shoulder. "I am so glad to have someone to travel with, Nathan."

He could feel the warmth of her body through the many layers of fabric between her skin and his. That was enough to give him a hard-on.

Amanda looked down at the bulge in his trousers. The girl's eyes went wide and she reached down to touch him there.

Longarm damn near jumped out of his skin when she placed her hand on the lump caused by his rigid cock.

She turned her face up to him and giggled. "Do you mind?"

"Uh . . . no, I reckon not."

"I've heard about these thing," Amanda mused, "but I've never seen one. Would it be all right if I see yours? See it and maybe . . . more than just see?"

"Not setting here in this railcar with other folks passing by, you ain't."

"Later then. Would that be all right, Nathan? Please?"

He patted her arm. And smiled.

Chapter 5

"Why is the train slowing down?" She leaned in close against him and laid her hand on his arm when she spoke. He could not say that he minded being so close; she was an awfully pretty little thing.

"End o' the line," Longarm said. "The Denver and Rio Grande only goes as far as El Moro. The Santa Fe line was the right of way on south from here. They've built past Trinidad but not very far yet."

"How will we get south then?"

"Stagecoach. They run from Trinidad on down. Are you going far?"

"Las Vegas. Have you heard of it?"

Longarm nodded. "Heard of it, yes." Been there many times, too, but that was as a federal lawman and not a traveling businessman. "You have people there?"

Amanda said, "I have a sister there. Amy is married now and in the family way. Mama is sending me down to help her until she has the baby. If I know Amy, that will mean the two of us sitting in rocking chairs for the next four or five months, tatting or sewing or knitting or such. And with nothing to talk about. Can you think of anything more boring than that?" She sniffed. "Amy and I never got along all that well when she lived at home. I declare, I don't know what Mama was thinking of to send me down here like this. It is an exile, that's what it is." She looked up at Longarm and giggled. "But I'll bet you can give me something to remember while I sit there with a ball of yarn in my lap."

"You sound serious, girl."

"I am. Really, really serious. When we get to Trinidad or Raton or one of those places we could get a room. Don't worry, I'll pay my half. Papa gave me money to travel on. Twenty dollars. That should be enough, don't you think?"

"You're too young," he objected.

"I'm twenty years old. Come November I'll be twenty-one. That is certainly old enough to know my own mind."

"You're a virgin," he said.

"But I won't be for much longer. I can promise you that much. I will not spend this whole time with Amy and go home still a virgin. If I have to I'll ... I'll ... I will find some man on the street and proposition him."

"You can't be serious. That would be dangerous. You could be beaten or robbed or get a disease. Do you even know about the diseases you can get from, uh, that?"

"No. Should I?"

"Damn right you should. An' wouldn't that be a fine mess. One o' these days when you meet the man you marry, you could pass the disease along to him. What would he think of his pretty little bride if she gave him the clap or the crabs or something even worse?"

"I don't know what those things are," Amanda said.

"An' I hope you never have t' find out about them. No, this idea that you got to get shut of your cherry, it ain't good."

"You could teach me though. You look like a man who would be gentle."

"Huh. That just goes t' prove that you're a lousy judge o' men. I'm rough on a woman. Use 'em and throw 'em away, that's me."

Amanda laughed and clapped her hands. "But that is

perfect, Nathan. I don't want a relationship. I want an introduction to the act of physical love. Nothing more. And I think . . ." She lowered her eyes and blushed. "I think I would like it rough. A little, anyway. I want . . . I've been pampered my whole life. Now I want to feel like a real woman. Do you hear what I'm saying? A *real* woman."

"You're a hard girl t' turn down."

Amanda sighed. "You don't have to do me, of course. If you prefer, I can look for someone in Trinidad who would take me. I should be able to find someone in one of the saloons, wouldn't you think? A cowboy or a coal miner. Perhaps a sheepherder. Do you think I should offer to pay a man for, well, for that?"

"Damnit, girl, I ought spank you," Longarm snapped.

Amanda's eyes sparkled. "Yes. I've never been spanked before. I think I should be. With your belt? Or do you have a razor strop in your bag? Spank me good, Nathan. I'm asking you, please."

Lordy, Longarm thought. If she walked into some honky-tonk with that attitude the girl could wind up dead in a ditch.

"You will take me, Nathan. Won't you?" Her eyes were big and blue and lovely.

"In Trinidad," he said. "We'll share a room. Then tomorrow we'll take a stage to Las Vegas, but once we get there you don't know me an' I don't know you no more. Is that a deal?"

She giggled. "Deal," she said, putting her gloved hand out for him to shake again.

Chapter 6

Nothing more had been said about Amanda's virginity, and by the time the train screeched and clanked to a halt Longarm was convinced the girl had only been teasing him. Which was something of a pity because she was a toothsome little thing.

She peered out the window and frowned. "This doesn't look like much of a town."

Longarm laughed. "That's because it isn't. This here is El Moro. It was created from bare prairie by the Denver and Rio Grande with the idea that folks would want t' come here an' stay just because the railroad was here. They figured all the businesses down in Trinidad would move up here t' be close to all the trade the railroad would bring in. 'Cept the Santa Fe line came along so Trinidad kinda has its own railroad, and the D and RG was left hanging. El Moro turned out t' be nothing more than a transfer point for folks going on further south. An' that's what you an' me need t' do now is to transfer. D'you have a lot o' baggage?"

"Two bags and a small trunk is all. Papa said I should travel light."

Longarm rolled his eyes. "All right then. We'll get a porter with a hand truck an' let him handle it all." He motioned for the next porter in line and told the girl, "Give the man the baggage token they handed you when you checked your bags in."

When the fellow stopped beside them Longarm handed him a brass disk with a number on it. Amanda gave him hers. "Yes, sir. Right away, sir." The porter bobbed his head and chuckled—attractive girl, handsome man, two separate baggage checks but leaving the train together; yes, sir, indeed—and said, "I'll bring 'em right up. The coaches, they're right over there." He pointed toward a line of waiting rigs—former army ambulances, Longarm saw at a glance—ready to take passengers the short distance down to Trinidad.

"Could we ride in that one?" Amanda asked.

"Sure. They're all about the same. Why this one?"

The girl laughed. "I like the look of the horses, that's all."

"Fair enough reason," Longarm said. He handed her into the back of the wagon and stood outside to make sure the porter got the right bags aboard, then paid both the porter and the coachman once the chore was accomplished. The coachman asked, "Where to, sir?"

"We'll be needing a hotel," Longarm told him. "Something clean and decent, not too expensive."

"I know just the place. Climb in." Fifteen minutes later the driver brought them to a halt outside a two-story structure close to the Santa Fe tracks. "Clean, decent, and not too expensive, just like you said."

Longarm enlisted the services of two muscular teenage boys to handle the baggage, then went in and registered them as Mr. and Mrs. Nathan James.

"Can we have supper first?" Amanda asked.

"Nervous?"

She bobbed her head. "A little."

"You don't have t' do it at all, you know. You can change your mind any time you want."

"I want to. Really I do. It's just . . . I'm nervous. You know? Scared."

"You'll be fine. Come along downstairs. We'll have something to eat and then, um, turn in for the night just like any married couple. Which we are." He winked at her. "For tonight anyhow."

"I don't know that I could eat anything," she said. Then proceeded to pack away enough grub to feed three men for a week.

The next time they went up to their room Longarm made a point of locking the door behind them. Then he took Amanda into his arms and spent some serious time kissing her. That, he was sure, was something she would have plenty of experience with.

He eased her down onto the thin quilt spread over the double bed and began unfastening the buttons on her dress.

Chapter 7

The girl had a lovely body. Slim and sleek with the vitality of youth. Her skin was smooth and supple as silk, and her pubic hair was as soft as thistledown.

Her belly fluttered with nervous anticipation when he bent his head to it and kissed her there.

Amanda's breasts were firm and well formed. They stood tall even when she lay on her back. Her nipples were small and pink, perching like tiny, sharp-tipped cones on top of her tits.

He kissed those too and lingered there for a while until she began to moan and to writhe.

"Beautiful," he told her reassuringly. "Beautiful."

Abruptly, Amanda sat up. She pushed him away at arm's length and took a deep breath.

"It's all right," he told her gently. "You're scared, that's all. We can stop here."

"No, silly. I don't want to stop. God knows, I don't ever want to stop feeling like that. I want more. Lots more. But first I want to get a good look at you." She leaned forward and kissed him. "You did promise, you know."

"Ayuh, so I did." Longarm stood and quickly stripped out of his clothes, laying everything piece by piece over a chair that sat beside the chest of drawers in the plain but impeccably clean hotel room. When he was done he stood in front of Amanda and let her look him over. After a moment he turned around so she could get that view, too. When he turned back again his erection was so thoroughly engorged with blood that it bounced with every beat of his heart. He peeled back his foreskin, going slowly and allowing Amanda to observe what he was doing. Her eyes were wide with wonder, but she did not speak.

"Is it what you expected?" he asked.

"What? Oh! I'm . . . sorry. I was distracted."

Longarm smiled. "Yeah, I noticed. Look it over good. You can touch it if you want."

She was hesitant at first, but her curiosity got the better of her reluctance. Amanda very gently touched the shaft and ran her fingertips up and over the red, bulbous head. "Oh, my. It . . . it looks like it should be as hard as china, but the feel of it is like velvet. Soft and smooth and . . . ooo! I like it." She laughed.

"Kiss it," Longarm suggested.

"What? Are you serious?"

"Of course. It's only skin, you know."

Amanda leaned forward. She breathed in deeply, apparently taking in the scent that came off Longarm's flesh. Then, very lightly, she touched her pursed lips to the side of his shaft.

"Are they all this big?" she asked.

Longarm shrugged. "I dunno. I ain't seen all o' them."

Amanda laughed and leaned forward again. This time she let her tongue run over his cock, and it was Longarm's turn to shiver.

"Does that feel good?" she asked.

"Damn right it does, girl. Listen, d'you want me t' teach you how to suck cock so that you drive a man plumb crazy?"

Her eyes went wide. "You could do that?"

"I could sure try. One thing, though. If you're gonna do

this, you are gonna learn to do it right. That means swallowing my jism."

"Jism? What is that?"

"You don't know . . . oh, darlin', are you ever in need o' some learning." Longarm sat beside her on the edge of the bed. He took her hand in his and moved it to his stiffly upright cock. "Don't be in a hurry now," he said. "We got all night long if need be, but do pay attention. First thing, you need t' learn the basics, like what a cock is all about. Then I'll teach you what t' do with it. So pucker up an' give me a kiss, right there on the tip end of it. Then I'll show you what feels the best to a man an' how you can go about driving any fella purely out of his mind."

Chapter 8

"Remember now," Longarm said as they waited for a porter to come take their bags downstairs, "once we get outta this room we're only two people that happen t' be traveling in the same direction. We ain't acting married nor like lovers, none of that. We're just strangers."

"Do I have to?" Amanda complained, rising on tiptoes to give him a deep kiss with the tip of her tongue playing over his lips and challenging Longarm's tongue.

"Yes, you have to," he said.

"You sound so gruff when you say that."

"That's because I'm a mean son of a bitch," he said sternly. Then he grinned and added, "I get that way every time I have t' go without sleep."

"Have to, was it?" she returned. "I don't remember you worrying about sleep last night."

"There were more interesting things happenin' at the time," Longarm told her. And there had been. The girl was a fast learner, at least when it came to matters of the human body and how best to give one pleasure. She was a more-than-fair fuck and could suck cock like a suction machine. Longarm doubted either one of them had gotten twenty minutes of sleep the whole night long.

A porter took their bags away with instructions to deposit them at the Atchison, Topeka & Santa Fe depot, then Longarm and Amanda were free to find a café—there was one two doors down from the hotel—and have breakfast.

After that there was ample time to explore the shops of Trinidad—something Amanda found much more enjoyable than Longarm did—and catch the next southbound train for the very short run to the end of the still-under-construction Santa Fe tracks. There they transferred to a stagecoach pulled by six powerful draft horses for the climb up to Raton Pass. At the town of Raton they stayed with the same coach but the team was changed to a lighter four-up for the downhill run and on south through Springer and Wagon Mound and eventually to Las Vegas.

They and four other sleepy passengers arrived in Las Vegas in the middle of the night. Longarm helped Amanda down from the coach and let her tug him into the shadows while the team was being changed out.

She wrapped her arms around his waist and gave him a surprisingly strong hug, laying her face on his chest and sighing. "I know you'll forget me soon enough, Nathan, but I'll never my whole life long forget you. Never," she whispered.

He smiled and kissed her. "You're wrong about that, lass. I'll not be forgetting you. Not never." He pulled away from her and said, "Come along now. You need to collect your bags, and I don't think there is anyone here to meet you. Do you know how to find your sister?"

"Yes, I think so."

"Think so?"

"I know I can. Don't worry about me now. I'll be fine." She giggled. "Bored maybe, but fine." In a louder, firmer voice she said, "Thank you for watching out for me, Mr. James. You've been very kind." Then she extended her gloved hand for him to lightly shake. Longarm glanced around and saw the stage line's swamper standing there.

"Your bags is all over there, ma'am. Is there anything else you'd be wanting?"

"Yes, could you find a hackney for me, please?"

Longarm turned away. Little Miss Amanda could take care of herself. He climbed back inside the coach and settled himself as comfortably as he could; it was still a very long way to El Paso.

Chapter 9

Longarm crawled slowly and painfully out of the damn coach. He had never been so glad to see any place as he was now to see El Paso. Two and a half days of confinement in a succession of swaying, bouncing, bumping stagecoaches left him feeling like he had been beaten with sticks.

It was simply not logical that just sitting on his ass inside a moving conveyance would leave a man feeling so beat down and bone weary. But that was certainly the way Longarm felt at the moment.

He climbed down to the ground and stood on the sidewalk until his Gladstone was handed down off the roof rack, then he asked the express agent, "I could sure use a recommendation, friend. I'm needin' a place t' stay. Not no flop joint, mind you, but something on the cheap end o' things."

"You ever been to El Paso before?" the local fellow asked.

"No, sir, this is my first visit." That was a flat-out lie, of course. Longarm had been down south a number of times in the past and knew a few people including several of the Texas Rangers who were stationed in El Paso. But that was Custis Long. Businessman Nathan James had never been there before.

"I hear tell the Caldwell House is clean and not too expensive. Never stayed there myself, you understand, but I've heard good things about it. If you want to look it over, it's two blocks down and one block over."

"All right, thanks. Is there anything I should tell them about who it was as sent me?"

The express agent laughed and shook his head. "If you're thinking I'm sending you there so's I can get a kickback, that isn't it at all. Like I say, I've heard good things about it from folks passing through, that's all."

"All right, then. An' I truly do be thankin' you," Longarm said. He picked up his bag and headed that way. El Paso was a city of ten, maybe fifteen thousand souls. With any kind of luck Nathan James would not run into anyone who knew Custis Long.

And with luck he would not run into anyone, not anyone at all, for the next day or so. Under whatever name one cared to use, he intended to get that room and hole up until he'd had some sleep. He hadn't been in a bed in days. And then he hadn't bothered much with sleep.

He stifled a yawn and trudged slowly to the Caldwell House, signed the guest register as N. James, and paid five dollars—in advance—for a week's stay.

His second-floor room was small but scrupulously clean. It even had curtains swaying in the hint of breeze that came through the open window.

Longarm set his bag down, kicked off his boots, and dropped his jacket and gun belt on the bedside chair, then lay down without even bothering to disrobe.

He was asleep almost instantly.

Chapter 10

Longarm felt like shit when he came downstairs the next morning. And at that it was an improvement.

As it was he was bloated and puffy-eyed from sleeping so soundly. He badly needed a shave. He thought he was fairly close to starvation. Worst of all, he was out of cigars.

"Friend," he told the man on the desk, "I'm needin' a good meal, a shave, and a place where I can buy me some cheroots. All o' those, prob'ly in that order. What can you recommend to a traveling stranger?"

"For the breakfast, we got a dining room right here in the hotel, though this late in the morning you might have to settle for a lunch. But you can call it breakfast if you like. After that, there's a barber in the next block."

Longarm raised an eyebrow.

"That direction," the clerk said, pointing. "Then over a block and another block down there's a store where you can likely find some smokes."

"Is there a proper tobacconist nearby? I'm partial to particular brands."

"I know of one downtown but nothing close."

"All right then, thanks." Longarm preferred to avoid El Paso's downtown area where he might well run into someone who knew him. He would settle for inferior cigars rather than take that risk.

In the meantime . . . "What's the best way to get across into Mexico?"

The clerk smirked, probably thinking his guest would be going across the border in order to find one of the cheap and plentiful whores on the Del Norte side. "Just walk across the bridge. There's a penny toll for that. Or you can do what the Mexicans do; that's to go down into the river-bank and wade across. There's no charge for that. Coming back they'll ask you what country you're a citizen of. Just tell them you're an American and you can pass. But you do have to say the words or show some sort of identification that says you have the right to be here."

Longarm nodded. That much had not changed since the last time he was here.

"About that breakfast . . ."

"Right in here, Mr. James. Just follow me."

Half an hour later, with his belly full of pork chops and fried potatoes, deputy U.S. marshal Custis Long was feeling considerably better. He found the barbershop the hotel clerk had mentioned and took a seat among the handful of men who were waiting for their own morning shaves. After a tolerable wait it was Longarm's turn to use the chair.

The barber, a tall man with thinning gray hair and a nervous tic in his left eye, snapped his sheet with a flourish and spread it over Longarm's upper body, then moved around behind him to pin the sheet close around Longarm's neck. "What will it be today, friend?"

"A shave is all."

"Really? You could use a trim. Make you look fine for the ladies." Longarm could hear a smile in the man's voice. "Especially after I splash on some bay rum."

"Now how is a man s'posed t' resist a sales pitch like that?" Longarm asked with a laugh.

"Ah, that's the point. You aren't. So, would you like the

haircut? It's only fifteen cents more when you combine it with the shave."

"You, sir, are a highwayman. A robber. But a good barber, as I've noticed on those other fellas before me." Longarm grinned. "Yes, damnit, give me the works. Including the bay rum."

Longarm closed his eyes and pretended to doze. In fact he was following the conversations around him, hoping someone would talk about the Chinese who were said to be coming into the country. No one did, however, and all he got out of the deal was the shave and a very good haircut.

When he left the chair he paid the barber for his services and tipped the man a nickel, then retrieved his hat from the rack and headed out into the midday sunshine.

Now he needed those cigars.

And a saloon where a fellow might be able to do a little eavesdropping without being obvious about it.

Chapter 11

"One o' those pickled sausages would be nice. And another beer. Thanks." Longarm laid down his nickel and picked up a soda cracker to go with the mouth-puckeringly sour sausage. He took a bite, picked up his beer mug, and moved a few feet down the bar so he would not block the way of the next fellow who might want a bit of the free lunch spread.

A burly man with a full beard and derby hat carved a chunk of cheese off the block of it provided there, bought himself a beer, and moved over beside Longarm. The fellow took a long drink, carefully wiped his hands on his vest and extended his right to Longarm to shake.

"Don't believe I've seen you in here before, friend," he said.

"No, sir, I'm new here," Longarm admitted.

"I'm Jake Newton. I deal in real estate. House, lots, land holdings of various sorts. If there's anything you need, all you have to do is ask for Jake. I can take care of it for you."

Longarm smiled, nodded, shook hands. "I'm Nathan James, down here looking to hire some cheap labor, which I've heard tell is available in these parts." It was the story he had decided to spin, hoping that it might lead him to the Chinese.

"Pleasure to meet you, Mr. James."

"Nathan, please. There's no need t' be formal, Mr. Newton. Not with me, there ain't."

Newton smiled. "Then you should call me Jake, Nathan. Say, do you mind if I ask you something?"

"Anything," Longarm said.

"Your name being James, I was wondering, are you any kin to the famous outlaws of that name?"

"Not that I know of," Longarm said and proceeded to go through the rest of his disclaimer. He was beginning, though, to think that he had chosen unwisely when he named himself after Frank and Jesse James. It was too late to change it now. His bank drafts were in the name of Nathan James and so was his telegraph address in Denver in case he needed to contact Billy Vail or Henry.

"So you could be related," Newton persisted after Longarm had completed his denial of any known relationship.

Longarm shrugged. "Could be, I suppose, but distant if at all."

"That's interesting. I see your glass is empty. Can I buy you another?"

"That's mighty nice o' you, Jake."

"It will be my pleasure, Nathan." He raised his voice and called, "Herm. Two more over here, please. Say, boys, come over here and meet a man who might be kin to Jesse James. This here is Nathan James. Nathan, these gents are . . ." Newton ran through a quick list of introductions to others who obviously were frequent customers in Herman Johnson's Topeka Saloon.

Within seconds Nathan James was accepted as one of the boys in the Topeka. Longarm smiled and bobbed his head and bought a round of drinks for everyone.

Chapter 12

Oh, *shit*!

Standing there minding his own business, buying a few beers and keeping his ears open, the next thing he knows he looks up and sees Texas Ranger Dan Congdon walking toward him. Congdon and Longarm had worked together for several weeks, an investigation up in the Texas panhandle that led to the arrest and conviction of a gang of stagecoach holdup men. Boys, really. Not a one of them over eighteen but their pistols had been full grown. That was—Longarm tried to recall—two years ago? Two and a half?

He and Congdon had worked well together. Longarm liked and respected the ranger. But he had *not* wanted to run into the fellow here in El Paso now.

It was too late to duck his head and turn away, Longarm saw. Dan already saw him and was coming straight toward him, the beginnings of a smile tugging at his lips and his hand ready to extend for the obligatory shake.

"Cus . . ."

Longarm punched his friend in the mouth hard enough to take Dan off his feet.

"Don't you be cussing me, damn you," Longarm said loudly, trying to slur his words a little so it would seem he was beginning to get drunk. "I told you before t' leave me alone." Hopefully the men standing around the Topeka would assume "Nathan James" and Dan Congdon had had harsh words already.

"What the hell?" Congdon snapped, climbing to his feet after being decked by Longarm's hard right hand. "Why, Cus . . ."

Longarm hit him again. He did not want Dan to get his name out. He was Nathan James, damnit, not Custis Long, not Longarm . . . *Nathan James*!

Congdon went sprawling, back onto the sawdust-littered floor.

"I don't know who you are, mister, but I'm not gonna stand here an' let you cuss me. No, sir, I ain't."

Congdon came into a crouch and felt of his jaw, then stood. "I'll cuss you as much as I like," the ranger declared, "and I'll arrest your scrawny ass, too, if I take a mind to. You obviously don't know it, but I'm a Texas Ranger and I have the power to put you behind bars until you sober up."

"Fuck you," Longarm snarled. "I dare you to 'rest me. You ain't man enough t' get that job done."

"I'll show you who's man enough. Now turn around and put your hands behind your back. You're going to jail, mister."

"Like hell I am," Longarm declared.

"Like hell you aren't," Congdon shot back at him.

"You go t' hell." Longarm blinked, swayed back and forth a bit and took another punch at Dan Congdon, this one sailing well wide of the mark and hitting nothing but thin air.

Congdon retaliated with a blow to Longarm's short ribs and a punch to the jaw hard enough to make Longarm see stars.

Longarm grunted, dropped to one knee, and held still long enough for Congdon to whack him again. This time

Longarm toppled to the floor, then groggily pushed himself up to hands and knees.

"That's it, damnit," he heard Congdon bark. He felt his hands being pulled behind his back and the bite of steel bracelets being snapped around his wrists. "You, mister, are on your way to the pokey."

Dan Congdon jerked Longarm to his feet and bodily hauled him out the door.

Congdon hailed a hansom cab and had them delivered to the city jail, the El Paso ranger station not having a lockup of its own.

"Sorry about that, Custis," Dan Congdon said as he unlocked the handcuffs on Longarm's wrists. "I didn't mean to hang you out in the breeze."

Longarm looked around.

"We're alone in here," Congdon assured him. They were in a small interrogation room inside the jail.

"Hope I didn't hurt you none, Danny boy," Longarm said as he rubbed his wrists. Those handcuffs had been tight. And the steel didn't stretch worth a damn.

"You? A weakling like you hurt me?" Congdon snorted. "That'll be the day."

"You understand, I hope, that I couldn't let you get my name out. Right now my name is Nathan James an' I'm down here on a job. Know anything about Chinese coming across the border from Mexico, Danny?"

"What the hell? Is Mexico closing down all their laundries? That would be, what, six or seven Chinamen out of work."

"There's s'posed t' be a quota, but somebody's bringing in a whole lot more. The attorney general, or maybe it's some senators, are all hot an' bothered about it, so some o' us have been told to go find out what's going on. I guess there's a bunch o' new laws in the works about it." Longarm grinned. "If you ever read the newspapers, you'd know all that shit. Assuming you can read, that is."

Congdon laughed. "You're still a son of a bitch, Custis."

"You haven't changed much yourself, Danny."

"What can I do to help?" the Texas Ranger asked.

"Apart from keeping your clumsy ass outta my way, you mean?"

"Yeah, aside from that."

"Now that I think about it, Dan, since I been seen coming in here drunk an' in 'cuffs, or so I hope it looked anyhow, now that I been seen being hauled inside here, I think it might be a good idea for you t' put me in the tank overnight. Book me in like any other prisoner. Hell, that'd give me a chance t' meet some o' El Paso's less desirable citizens. Might be just what I need."

"That will be a pleasure," Congdon said with a smile. "Yes, sir, throwing your ass in jail will sure be a pleasure. What did you say your name is again?"

Chapter 13

"Son of a bitch hotel specializes in cockroaches, don't it," Longarm growled. He stomped a bug that was skittering across the floor, then stood inside the cell rubbing his wrists where the handcuffs had chafed them.

"What're you in for?" someone asked.

The cell was a large holding tank perhaps ten by twenty-some feet. Steel benches lined the walls. At the moment it held six men other that Custis Long.

Longarm shrugged. Then grinned. "'Cause I busted one of those smart-ass son-of-a-bitch rangers square in the mouth an' knocked him on his ass, that's why."

"Why'd you go an' do a thing like that?"

"Shit, I dunno. It seemed a pretty good idea at the time."

"Drunk and disorderly," another prisoner put in.

"That's what they called it," Longarm said. "I thought I was fine. Still do."

"My name is Jim Craddock," the second man said, rising to his feet and extending his hand.

"How do, Jim. I'm Nathan James."

A third man spoke. "James, eh? You any kin to Jesse?"

Longarm went through his by now well-worn story

about not being sure if he was related to the famous James
brothers.

The rest of the men in the cell crowded near, obviously
curious about this man who might—or might not—be related to Frank and Jesse James. All the men, that is, except
one ragged and destitute bum who was stretched out on the
floor reeking of liquor and puke and softly snoring.

The others, Longarm noticed, appeared to be cowboys in
town to raise some hell and have a good time. Most looked
more or less battered by their fun. The only exception was
Jim Craddock, whose appearance was that of . . . Longarm
tried to guess . . . certainly some sort of businessman, perhaps a livestock buyer. Craddock's boots were those of a
horseman, and Longarm could see the marks on the heels
where spurs usually rubbed the leather.

He could see, too, the distortions on Craddock's belt
where the straps of some sort of contraption, probably a
shoulder holster, would normally be tugging the tooled
leather out of shape.

Craddock was almost as tall as Longarm with wavy black
hair and hazel eyes. He was clean shaven, or had been not
more than a day or two ago. His clothes suggested he was no
bum. Far from it. He seemed to have money to spend on
good quality cloth and a tailor who knew what to do with it.

Longarm walked to the side of the cell away from the
sleeping drunk and sat. The gray steel bench was icy cold
when he sat on it and the longer he stayed there the harder
it got. After a while he got up and walked to the front of the
cell and peered out through the bars.

"Depressing, isn't it."

Longarm looked. It was Craddock who had come over
to stand beside him.

"It's not a view I'd enjoy for long," Longarm agreed.
The only thing to see outside their cell was a gray steel
corridor leading, in one direction, to the administration area
and in the other toward the cells allotted to prisoners who

had already been sentenced. The holding tank where Longarm and his current companions found themselves was only used until a man had been arraigned.

"We'll see the magistrate tomorrow morning around six thirty," Craddock said. "He's a part-time judge, you see. He has a job selling furniture the rest of the time so he comes in early to take the arraignments and easy pleas. Serious charges are bound over for Judge Dahlenberg and the lawyers to yap about."

"Is there anything I ought to know?"

Craddock nodded. "Keep your mouth shut and say 'sir' a lot. If you try to deny you should be here or to make excuses, you'll draw anywhere from three to ten days. If you stay quiet and contrite . . . you know the word?"

"Of course," Longarm said.

Craddock grunted. "Like I was saying, keep your mouth shut and act sorry. For D and D . . . this your first-time offense?"

Longarm nodded.

"That's an easy one. In that case as long as you're sober when you get in front of him, he'll sentence you to time served . . . that means tonight . . . and turn you loose tomorrow morning."

"That seems painless enough," Longarm said. "What about you, Jim? Why are you enjoying the hospitality of the city?"

A smirk tugged at Craddock's lips. He hesitated for only a moment, then said, "I had a little altercation with one of the whores over at Le Bistro. Bitch claimed I hit her." Craddock grunted. "Next time I'll beat the shit out of her."

"What will you get for that?"

"Oh, three days, maybe five. Not much anyway. Hell, it was only a whore. Mexican whore at that. If it'd been a decent white woman, I'd have been bound over for trial in front of Dahlenberg and got at least a month and probably a whole lot more."

"You seem to know what to expect," Longarm said.

"I pay attention," Craddock said. "I read the newspapers and I observe. You wait and see if I'm not right about this."

"You seem like the sort of man who knows what is what," Longarm said. He smiled. "D'you smoke, Jim? Would you like a cigar?"

Chapter 14

"Hey! You!"

Longarm stopped, cheroot in hand, and turned his head. "Me?"

"That's right, asshole. You." The belligerent fellow who was barking at Longarm was a squat, heavily muscled man whose salt-encrusted dungarees and sun-blackened skin suggested day after day working outdoors. The man was a head shorter than Longarm and half again wider. It was not until he stood up and approached Longarm and Craddock that Longarm saw he had only one arm, his left. At this moment he did not look happy.

"What's your problem?" Longarm asked.

"You. Don't you know the rule, asshole?"

"I got no idea what rule you'd be talking about," Longarm returned. It was a completely honest answer.

"Rule is, mister, whatever you got, you share. If you're gonna give him a smoke, you gotta give me one, too. And these other fellas if they want one."

"Friend, I don't mind sharing, but I've only got these two an' one I figure to have tonight," Longarm said. He thought it was a reasonable enough explanation. Obviously that was a minority opinion because now the rest of the prisoners were paying attention and acting like they too might like a good cigar courtesy of this latest arrival.

"You can go without, asshole. Now gimme that cigar. I didn't have none on me when I was picked up by those chickenshit police so I'll just take that one."

"You know," Longarm said, "if you had come over here and asked could you please have one o' my smokes, I woulda give it to you. But you can stand there all damn day demanding that I give up my own property to you an' all you'll get is exercise for your jaws. Now fuck off before I forget what a short little son of a bitch you are an' squash you like a bug."

Longarm noticed that the other prisoners were paying attention now. They began to close in behind the one-armed man. They were grinning.

"I'm gonna whip your ass," the squat fellow declared.

"Mister, you got only one arm. I can't fight you. Wouldn't be fair," Longarm said.

"Well, I'm gonna fight you whether you fight me or not."

"Wouldn't be fair," Longarm insisted.

"You're the only one worrying about fair," the small man returned.

"If you're going to fight him," Jim Craddock put in, "let me hold those cigars so they don't get busted in the scrap."

Longarm grunted. And handed over the three cheroots he had happened to have in his shirt pocket when Danny "arrested" him. He turned back to the one-armed man. "I'm still not gonna fight you."

"Bullshit," the fellow said, then lowered his head and charged.

Son of a bitch used his head as a battering ram. And a damned well powerful ram at that.

He hit Longarm in the breadbasket and drove the breath from him. Longarm tried to grapple with him but wound up grabbing at the fellow's empty sleeve instead.

Longarm tried to back away but his adversary kept boring in, the top of his head still firmly planted against Longarm's torso and his arm clamped like a vice around Longarm's waist.

Next Longarm tried punching the man, but at those close quarters the contest was a wrestling match, not a normal fight, and he could get no leverage against him.

The stocky, powerful fellow dropped down a bit, twisted . . . and lifted Longarm completely off his feet. Then he bulled forward at a sudden run, slamming Longarm against the wall and completing the job of driving the breath out of Longarm's lungs.

Another twist and Longarm went down, falling hard on one of the steel benches that lined the three walls where there were no bars.

Once he had Longarm on his back the one-armed man slid forward until his face was next to Longarm's.

The fellow whispered, "Watch yourself, mister. Craddock is a plant. He's really a copper with big ears. Don't tell him nothing you don't want a judge to hear." He put his hand in Longarm's face and pushed off, standing and leaving Longarm lying on the bench. In a loud voice he growled, "Now are you gonna share those cigars or ain't you?"

"You don't have t' get so worked up about it." Longarm stood, brushed himself off, and retrieved all three cheroots from Jim Craddock. He tucked all three back into his shirt pocket and sat by himself, well away from any of the other prisoners.

Chapter 15

"Time served." The judge's gavel banged down on his desk, and an El Paso city policeman who escorted the prisoners one by one before the judge tugged at Longarm's elbow and in a voice barely above a whisper said, "You're free to leave. Collect your things if you have any from the officer in charge of the jail."

"All right, thanks." Longarm left the courtroom and crossed the street to the city jail.

"You one of the prisoners?" a sloppy patrol officer with stains on his tunic asked.

"I was, but I ain't now," Longarm told him.

"Name?"

He very nearly slipped up and gave his real name but remembered in time and said, "Nathan James." In truth the alias was coming a little easier to him now.

"Oh, yeah. I seen your name on the log this morning. You mind if I ask you something?" Longarm said nothing so the policeman added, "Your name, mister. Are you related to Frank and Jesse?"

Longarm could have kicked himself for his choice of name now but once again he went through his standard reply.

No, he didn't know if he was actually kin to the famous brothers. But he could be.

"Yeah, well, I just wondered, that's all. Say, do you know if they're planning anything down this way?"

"I wouldn't know," Longarm said. "I've never met either one o' them."

The desk officer sniffed. Longarm got the impression the man did not believe his denial. And if the truth be told, Custis Long did not give a crap if the officer believed him or not. "My stuff?" he prompted.

"What? Oh, right. Let me check, uh . . ." The man bent over some papers, shuffled several to the bottom of the stack and brought others up. Wrote in two different ledgers. Finally he said, "Sign this." He shoved a form across the desk to Longarm, then stood and disappeared into a back room. Moments later he returned with a box that was perhaps a foot wide and two feet long but only six or seven inches deep. He set the box on his desk, looked at the form and complained, "You haven't signed it. Can't sign your own name, eh?"

"I haven't signed it because it says I received all my property back from you and that it is in the same condition as when I gave it to you."

"That's right, so what's the problem?"

"The problem is that I haven't received anything back yet."

"Your things are all in this box. So is the inventory you signed when it was taken from you."

"Let me look them over. If it's all there and hasn't been messed with, *then* I'll sign your damned form."

"Don't get snippy with me, mister. I'll put your ass right back in that cell and you can spend a few more nights behind bars if you like."

What Longarm would have liked would be to sink his fist about elbow deep into this asshole's belly, but he doubted that would accomplish much.

He checked through the box and retrieved his money—it was all there, surprisingly enough—and strapped his gun belt on, taking plenty of time to make sure it was set just exactly so. Then and only then did he lean down and sign the form to certify that everything indeed had been returned to him.

"Thank you a whole hell of a lot," Longarm grumbled, then turned and strode out of there.

He paused on the sidewalk to look around and make sure of where he was. When he did he heard someone behind him.

"You," he said. The one-armed man was leaning against the front wall of the jail.

The fellow grinned and rubbed his chin.

"I figured by now you'd be having a drink. Or a woman. Or both," Longarm told him.

"I woulda been, too, except for you, mister. I'd like to have a word with you if you aren't in a hurry."

Longarm shrugged. "I got nothin' better t' do right now so you lead the way an' I'll be right behind you."

Without another word the one-armed man started off down the street at a rapid pace.

Chapter 16

Longarm expected the one-armed man to take him to a saloon or a café where they could talk. Instead they left the businesses several blocks behind and passed through a gate leading to a small house with bright colored flowers growing in large pots on the front porch.

The fellow opened the door without knocking and motioned for Longarm to go inside, then followed him into the shaded and much cooler interior.

"In there," he said, pointing to a tidy parlor to the left of the entrance. Then he raised his voice and called, "Bobbi. Where the hell are you?"

"In here. I'm in the kitchen," a woman's voice answered.

"Good, because I'm hungry. I want something to eat. There's two of us."

"Who'd you drag home this time?"

"None of your business." He turned to Longarm and said, "Sorry about that." He extended his hand to shake and finally got around to introducing himself. "I'm Bob Temple. In the jail I heard them say your name is James?"

"That's right. Nathan James." Longarm shook Temple's hand. "Your wife name is Bobbi?"

"Aw, she's not my wife. If I was going to get married,

I'd pick something with tits. No, that one's my sister. Our folks had a sense of humor, I suppose. Or thought they did. Bob and Bobbi. Robert and Roberta actually." He raised his voice again. "Hurry up with that lunch, will you."

"You got two choices," the female voice came back. "Shut up or go find your own meal."

Temple turned to Longarm and shrugged. "She's got a temper. Comes by it honestly enough, I suppose, because I got one, too. Which is why I was in jail. Fighting. We've got so the magistrate and me have a sort of understanding. He knows I'm going to fight. I get picked up for it and he always sentences me to time served. Which is fine unless I get picked up on a weekend and have to spend more than just the one night in there. I always try to keep my fist to myself on Friday nights." He laughed. "Can't always do it, mind, but I try. You were in for fighting, too?"

Longarm nodded.

"It speaks well of a man if he won't take crap off anybody. That's why I gave you some shit about those stupid cigars. I didn't really want one, but I wanted to check you out a little and warn you about that cop Craddock. I know about him, you see, because I been in that damned jail so often. He spends a lot of time there, too, enough to draw my attention. He always tells the same story about beating up on some Mexican whore. I doubt he's got the balls to know what a Mexican whore looks like, much less to make 'em squeal." Without pausing for a breath Temple raised his voice again and shouted, "Damnit, Bobbi, where's our lunch?"

"Don't you be using language like that with me, Robert Buell Temple, or I'll rip your last arm off of you and smack you over the head with it. Now come in here and set down to the table like gentlemen, the both of you."

Longarm was no longer sure he wanted to have lunch with these people. Hell, it might not be safe to.

On the other hand, he had not had supper last night nor

breakfast this morning. And the scents coming through that kitchen door were mighty enticing.

He could stay, he decided, but just for a little while. Just long enough to have a bite of that lunch.

Chapter 17

If he had put fifty men into a room and fifty women with them, he never would have been able to pair Bob and Bobbi Temple as brother and sister. Hell, if he had put two people into a room, and those two being them, he *still* would not have been able to figure them for brother and sister.

Bob was built like a bull, short and thick and burned back by the sun. Bobbi was tall and skinny, her hair pale and her complexion washed out. She had to be the same age as Bob, the two of them being twins, but she looked ten years older. And like he had hinted the woman had no tits. The front of her dress hung as smooth and flat as if she were a boy.

The question here, though, was whether she could cook. Custis Long was prepared to testify that she damn sure could.

With Bob gobbling from one side of the table and Longarm stuffing himself from the other, the two of them managed to lay waste to one chicken, a platter of pork chops, and a good-sided bowl of spicy Mexican beans. Longarm doubted he had ever been so hungry. Or so pleased with any meal. Bobbi Temple knew which end of a spatula to hold on to.

"Ma'am," he told her when he finally shoved his plate

away and refused the last pork chop, "you're as fine a cook as ever I've knowed. Thank you."

She blushed a furious shade of red as she poured a refill into Longarm's coffee cup.

"Don't be tell her shit like that," her brother advised. "You'll swell her head something terrible."

"You shut up, Robert."

Longarm knew when to hold his water. He crossed his arms and clamped his mouth shut and stayed out of the family bickering.

"You best be the one to shut up or you know what you'll get next." Unable to use knife and fork to cut his meat, he simply picked up the last pork chop and chewed on it. By the time he was done the bone looked like it had been polished.

"Thanks for a fine feed," Longarm told Temple, sure the man's sister would be listening, too. "It really was as good as a man could hope t' find."

"I'm glad you liked it, Nathan. How's about you and me go into the parlor. There's something I want to talk to you about."

"Could we go out onto the porch instead?" Longarm asked. "I still have these cheroots in my pocket, an' I'd sure like t' smoke one."

"Sure. But keep your voice down out there. I got some business t' discuss with you if you don't mind."

Longarm nodded and pulled two cheroots from his pocket. He offered one to Bob, nipped the twist from his own and lighted both smokes before settling onto a cane-bottom rocking chair on the front porch.

The evening was cool and pleasant, and a very gentle breeze was blowing from the east. "Now tell me what's on your mind, Bob," he offered once both were comfortable.

By the time Bob Temple was done talking, Longarm's concerns about illegal Chinese immigrants and his own assignment from Washington had evaporated as completely as the puffs of smoke the two men exhaled into the evening air.

Chapter 18

The conversation had not gone the way Longarm expected, Temple having much more in mind than a shared meal. "Having only one arm can be a real pain in the ass," he admitted. "There's little things you just can't do, things most people wouldn't give a second thought to."

Temple rocked back in his chair and stayed there for a moment while he drew in smoke from the cigar Longarm had given him, then slowly exhaled. "Take a simple Mason jar, Nathan. Ever try opening one with one hand? It can be done, as I've had to learn, but it isn't easy. Opening a can of beans is worse. Sharpening a pencil. It's those little everyday things that drive you crazy."

"I wouldn't have thought about it," Longarm said, "but I can see that you be right, Bob."

"Some things I just can't do. Others I can get done but it takes me forever. You know what I'm saying? Putting harness on a horse, for instance. I can do that. Even learned to do the buckles one-handed, but it takes me half of forever."

"Makes sense that it would, I s'pose," Longarm said.

"Something else, something that I can't overcome," Temple said, "is how this makes me stand out. I mean, there's just not all that many men on the streets who only have one arm or one leg. We stand out in the crowd, don't you see."

"Aye, I do see that, Bob."

Temple rocked in silence for a time, smoking the cheroot until it was down to a nubbin, which he dropped into a large can sitting on the porch beside his chair. "I used to toss my butts in the yard," he explained, "but Bobbi, she has a damn hissy fit every time I do that. She comes along behind me and picks them up and then complains about the extra work for weeks afterward. It's easier just to use the can."

Longarm finished his own smoke, reached over, and dropped the butt into the can. He started to rise. "Thanks for everything, Bob. I . . ."

"Whoa. Hang on here a minute, will you, Nathan?"

Longarm stopped where he was, then settled back onto his rocker.

"I brought you here for a reason, Nathan. I have something planned out, but it's something I couldn't do myself, at least not by myself. You should understand that I have good taste. I like fine things. Expensive things. Whiskey, cigars, or women, I like quality goods." He turned his head away and sighed. "Not that you can tell it from what you see now."

"Money is hard t' come by," Longarm said.

"Don't I know it. I work hard for what I have. I drive a salt wagon. Go out onto the salt flats and load a wagon and trailer and bring the sale back here for another man to sell, mostly to markets over along the Gulf so they can salt fish and sell them on from there. But the profit from all that salt mostly goes to the leaseholder. It isn't my salt, you see. All I do is to haul it."

"That sounds like awful hard work."

"It is, Nathan. It's hard now and I'm not as young as I used to be. I still have my strength but I don't know for how long. I ache more the older I get, seems like."

Longarm smiled. "I know the feelin'."

"Back there in the jail, Nathan, you struck me as a man who likes quality every bit as much as I do."

"I like a good cigar and a fine whiskey, too, Bob. You nailed that."

"Let me be blunt with you, Nathan. Are you rich?"

"Me? Rich? Shit, no."

"That's what I thought. Now let me ask you something else. Would you like to be?"

"Rich? Would I like t' be rich?"

Temple nodded.

"Yes, o' course I would."

"You can be."

"You're shitting me, ain't you?"

"No, I am dead serious about this, Nathan. If we work together we could both be rich. And I'm not even sure it would be illegal, although it might be. Certainly some would consider it to be so."

"It's legal?" Longarm asked.

Temple shrugged. He held his hand out and rocked it back and forth. "Like I say, that depends on your point of view. Do you want to hear more?"

"Yes, Bob, I most definitely want to hear more about this idea," deputy United States marshal Custis Long said.

Chapter 19

Longarm climbed wearily up the stairs in the Caldwell House, found his room, and let himself in. After that night in the pokey he felt like he had soiled himself. Or that he had a host of tiny creatures crawling on his skin. He rang down to the desk for a bucket of hot water, sloshed half of it into the basin that sat on a washstand opposite the bed, and with soft soap and a sea sponge gave himself a bath there in the room.

He felt considerably better once he was clean. He found a clean shirt and clean balbriggans in his bag and got dressed, then rang downstairs again for the bellhop.

"D'you do laundry here, boy?"

"No, sir, but there's a Chinaman in the next block over. He does pretty good work."

"All right." Longarm bundled his dirty clothes into a wad and handed them to the freckle-faced kid. "Take these to him." He added a quarter to pay for the service, then lay down on the hotel bed. It felt good to have a proper mattress and bedsprings under him after the night on a hard steel bench in that jail cell.

He was down here to look into the smuggling of Chinese. The job Bob Temple wanted him to do had nothing to do with that problem.

Longarm sat upright on the bed as a thought came to him. It was true enough that he did not know of any connection between Temple's plan and the Chinese smuggling. But on the other hand, *he did not know that they were in fact not connected.*

Which as far as Custis Long was concerned meant he was free to string along with Temple on his deal.

String along for the time being, that is.

So far Robert Temple had his plans for a big heist. He wanted to hit a bank across the river on the Del Norte side, the Mexican half of El Paso, it being essentially one city that happened to straddle an international border and so lay in two different countries.

Common sense would suggest that Longarm arrest Temple. Except that common sense and the law are two different things. And while it might seem perfectly sensible to arrest Temple to stop him from pulling off this robbery, under the law a man cannot be arrested for something he has not yet done.

Besides, the bank Bob had chosen to hit was on the other side of the river. It was in a completely different country, completely different legal jurisdiction. Over in Del Norte, Custis Long had no more authority than Robert Temple did. His badge meant nothing there.

It was a dilemma. Longarm wanted to stop Bob from robbing that bank as a simple matter of right and wrong. Yet at the same time, he kind of liked the stocky little one-armed son of a bitch and hated the idea of sending him to prison for the next ten years or so. Especially in a Mexican prison.

If Longarm pulled out of the plan, Bob would only look for someone else with a full complement of limbs to help him rob the place.

If Longarm helped him, though, he would be derelict in his duty as a sworn peace officer.

After all, Longarm was pretty sure that Billy Vail would not look kindly on the idea of one of Billy's own deputies helping to pull off a heist. Not in Mexico and not anywhere else, either. Billy was picky about that sort of thing.

Longarm was in deep thought about it all, so deep that he began to snore.

Chapter 20

Longarm snatched his hat off and stepped back from the door. Bobbing his head, he said, "G'd'evenin', Miss Temple." He coughed into his fist, then held his cigar down by his side. "Is Bob to home?"

The woman shook her head. "I'm sorry, Mr. James. Bob was called out to a job this afternoon. He should be gone three days at the least, possibly longer. Is your inquiry urgent?"

"Oh, no, miss. I just figured t' talk with him, that's all, it can wait." All the better if it did, he realized. Some time during the next three days it was possible he might find a way out of this quandary he was in, not knowing how he should respond to Temple's invitation that Longarm help rob a bank across the border in Mexico. "Thank you, miss. When he gets back . . . um . . . tell him I was askin' for him, please."

"Of course I will, Mr. James."

"Yes, miss. Well . . . good evenin' then." Longarm took half a step backward, put his hat back on, and turned to go.

"Mr. James."

He stopped. Turned around. "Yes, miss?"

"I just put supper on the table. There is more than enough for two."

"That's nice o' you, miss, but I wouldn't want t' intrude."

"Please. It would be a pleasure to have someone to talk with. Bobby is gone so much of the time, and I have no friends here. It would be a kindness if you were to come in and share the meal with me."

"In that case, sure. Thank you." He had to eat some-where, he figured, and here he might get some ideas about how to get out of this business with Temple and hopefully do it without exposing himself as a lawman.

He followed Roberta Temple into the kitchen where the table was already laid for a solitary diner.

"Let me take that," she said, deftly lifting the Stetson from his hands. "Sit down right there." She pointed to the armchair at the head of the table. It was where Bob presumably would sit when he was home.

"I don't want to be a . . ."

"You'll be a pleasure, not a bother," she assured him, "Go on now. I'll bring your plate and things."

She did, quickly setting the place for him, pouring cof-fee, even loading a plate for him.

Longarm smiled. "I'm not used t' being waited on like this."

"It's my pleasure. Really."

The meal was as good as he remembered from earlier. If nothing else, Roberta was a fine cook. She ate only a few bites herself, concentrating on making sure Longarm was comfortable and satisfied. When he was done eating she said, "After dinner Bobby always likes to have coffee and a brandy. Would you like to move into the parlor? I'll bring them to you there. Take the big chair and put your feet up on the hassock. There is an ashtray if you would like to light that cigar I saw you sneak into your pocket earlier.

"I thought I got away with that," he confessed.

"Go on now. I'll bring your brandy and coffee." She shooed him away from the table and began moving their soiled plates into the sink and the leftover foods into the cold safe.

"You don't have to . . ."

"Go on now," she ordered. She ducked her head and blushed. "There is something, something I want to discuss with you later."

"All right then, but what . . . ?"

"Later," she said. "Let me get my nerve up first."

Longarm raised an eyebrow, not sure what she might mean by that. Get her nerve up for what?

Not that there was any sense in worrying about it. He would find out when the scrawny girl was ready.

Longarm picked up his coffee cup and carried it with him into the parlor.

Chapter 21

Longarm came awake with a snort and a toss of his head. He had been sleeping slumped low in Bob's armchair, his position cramped and awkward. Now he had a crick in his neck and a foul taste in his mouth. The stub of a cheroot lay in the ashtray beside him.

"Well hello, Sleepytime. Do you mind if I rename you that?"

"Bobbi. Jeez, I'm sorry. I didn't mean to . . . how long have I been asleep?"

"Don't apologize. It was a pleasure to have you here." She smiled. "For once a grown man wasn't trying to get away from me as quick as possible. With you lying there sleeping . . . I could make believe. You know?"

"Make believe about what?"

"Oh, silly things. Like pretending you and I were married and I could wait on you and take care of you and do everything to make you happy and comfortable. Like that."

She was still smiling, but there was a sadness behind her eyes. Longarm thought she might be on the verge of tears.

"I'm surprised you aren't married," he said. "No offense, but you're of an age when I would've expected it."

Bobbi gave him a startled look of genuine puzzlement and said, "You sound like you mean that."

"Of course I mean it," Longarm responded.

"I'm a plain woman, Nathan. Homely and plain. No man has ever looked at me . . . like that. Not really. Not with all these Spanish beauties in El Paso and Del Norte. I can't stand up to that sort of competition. So I make do with what I can find.

"Understand, please, I'm not claiming to be a virgin. If a man is too poor to buy a Mexican trollop, he can have me for nothing. That isn't any secret. Think of me like a public outhouse, always open for a quick dump."

"Bobbi, I . . . you shouldn't speak of yourself like that. From what I've seen of you, you're a wonderful woman. Caring and considerate. A fine cook and housekeeper. You're a really nice person, Bobbi. Don't talk down about yourself like that."

"But a fine, handsome man like you would never be interested in someone like me, Nathan. Not even for a quickie."

How the hell had he gotten himself backed into a corner like this, Longarm wondered. It was all too clear now where this conversation was headed, and he did not see any graceful way to get out of it. He sat up straight and rolled his head around a bit trying to get rid of the crick in his neck.

"Are you all right?" Bobbi asked.

Longarm nodded. "Just feeling sort of shitty after sleeping like that."

"No wonder. You were out for hours." The lamps in the parlor were burning now and there was darkness behind the curtains that covered the windows.

"Could I get something to drink? Something t' take this taste outta my mouth?"

"Of course. Whiskey?"

"That'd be fine."

"Or I have some nice cider you might like."

"Apple cider? Lordy, I haven't had any decent cider since I left West Virginia."

"That's where you're from, Nathan?"

"Yeah." He nodded again, a little surprised with himself for revealing his real origins. Bobbi was easy to talk to. He smiled. "That's a long time ago, though."

Bobbi hurried away to the kitchen. She was back moments later with a tumbler of a genuinely good cider, one that had the crisp, effervescent bite of fall in its flavor.

"This is good," Longarm said. It took the foulness from his mouth and seemed to clear the pounding in his head as well.

Bobbi knelt beside his chair. She took the tumbler from him and set it aside. Then she reached out and laid a hand on the bulge at the front of his trousers. She smiled at what she found there. "You are a big man, Nathan James."

"And you are a very forward young woman. I'm beginning to think you're the kind of girl who manages to get what she wants without making a big show of it."

Bobbi laughed. And began unbuttoning his fly.

Chapter 22

Bobbi appeared to be a very thin woman. That was when she was fully clothed. Naked, she was a skeleton with some skin draped over it. Longarm was not sure he had ever seen any healthy human being with so little flesh on their bones. Hell, it was a wonder she didn't clatter and clack when she walked.

Appearance had nothing to do with depth of passion, though. There was nothing lacking in Bobbi when it came to her desire to fuck. The girl just plain wanted to get laid, and she attacked Longarm's pecker like a scratch hen going after a worm. She dropped to her knees and practically inhaled him.

"Girl, I can't believe you're able t' take all that without choking," he said while he admired Bobbi's ability to suck cock. "Lordy, that do feel good." Which was entirely true. Not only could she take him deep into her throat, she did something with her tongue that damn near drove him wild.

While Bobbi was occupied on her knees, Longarm unbuttoned his shirt, stepped out of his balbriggans, and finished getting out of his clothes. Bobbi might not be pretty, but she made up for that in raw willingness.

"Here," he said once they both were naked, "stand up."

He reached down to cup her chin on his palm and lift her to her feet, wrapping an arm around her bony shoulders and bending his head to give the girl a kiss. He could feel her breath coming faster and she moaned softly, then shuddered.

Longarm bent, scooped Bobbi up, and asked, "Where's the bedroom?"

She inclined her head to point the way, and he carried her into the tiny, cluttered room that was dominated by a narrow, rumpled bed. When he placed her onto it he noticed that she was more than a little overdue to change the sheets.

"Oh, Nathan, you're a beautiful man, just beautiful." Beautiful was not a term that Custis Long thought of in connection with male humans. But then he was not a horny woman.

He lay beside and half on top of her and kissed her, long and thoroughly. Bobbi's breath was sweet to taste and she tried to suck his tongue down her own throat. Damned near did it, too, and likely would have if it had not been attached inside Longarm's mouth.

Running his hand up and down her body was like caressing a bundle of sticks, but from the way she squirmed and wriggled there was no doubt that she liked it more than a little bit.

He found her nipples, tiny little nubbins as dark as raisins and not much bigger. When he rolled them between his thumb and forefinger, Bobbi shuddered again and stiffened beneath his touch.

He bent his head to her right nipple and sucked it, gently nipped it with his teeth, and then licked it. Bobbi cried out as if in pain and once again shuddered and jerked to his touch.

"Girl, you aren't actually, uh . . . you know. Are you?"

"Yes. Yes, damnit, I am."

Longarm smiled. He did not think he ever knew a girl who was so quick to bring to a climax.

If she reacted like that to a few kisses and some nipple play, what would she do when he touched her pussy?

He decided to find out, his hand ranging south over the precipice of her rib cage, across the hollow flat of her quivering belly, and on into the scant bush of pubic hair between her legs.

It was certainly not difficult to find what he sought there. She was already dripping wet, the lips of her pussy gaping wide and hot for his searching finger.

Instead of shoving his hand up her twat, he played around at the entrance until he found the small, fleshy button of her clitoris. Bobbi immediately cried out and again came to a thunderous climax. She grabbed his hand with both of hers and pressed his fingers deep into herself, holding him there while she came yet again.

Longarm gave her plenty of time to finish what she was doing, then gently guided her hands to his throbbing dick.

Bobbi wrapped her fingers around him and sighed, then tugged him on top of her body, opening her legs to his entry.

Longarm let the girl position him above her, then lowered himself slowly into her wet, waiting flesh. He slid deep inside her, immersing himself in the heat of her body.

Bobbi wrapped herself tight around him, clinging with arms and legs alike and latching her mouth onto the side of his neck.

Longarm filled her body and held still there for long moments, letting Bobbi rock her hips ever so slightly until again she shuddered in a straining climax, the walls of her pussy contracting in rippling waves against his shaft when she came.

Time for his turn, he figured as he began to stroke in and out, slowly at first, but quicker then and deeper until he was pounding Bobbi's body with his own at a near-frantic pace.

Longarm exploded in a climax of his own, arching his back and driving deep inside her in one last, powerful convulsion of pleasure.

"Lordy," he whispered.

Bobbi hugged him. "Thank you, Nathan. Thank you." He was amazed to see that she was crying, her breath coming in sobbing gasps. "Thank you."

Longarm gave her a kiss and carefully moved off the girl. If he remained on top of her like that he was half afraid he might break some of those bones that were digging into him. Funny that he hadn't noticed the discomfort before.

"What can I get you, Nathan? What can I do for you?"

"I think you done me mighty well already, but truth is I wouldn't mind another glass o' that apple cider."

Bobbi squealed with joy at the idea she could do something for him and bounded off the bed to head for the kitchen and the jug of tasty cider.

Chapter 23

"Custis? Are you in here?"

"Over here, Dan. Just a second while I get a match. Then you can close the door and I'll give us some light." Longarm had found an abandoned adobe pig sty not far from the ranger headquarters. He sent a note to Dan Congdon by way of a Mexican kid and waited there for the ranger.

Longarm's match flared with a blaze of light and a whiff of burning sulfur. He held it aloft so Congdon could see to join him hunkered down on the edge of what had been a feed bunk.

"Nice place you found here," Congdon mused.

"Glad you like it." The match burned down to Longarm's fingers so he quickly shook it out then pinched the burned end to make sure there was no more fire before he dropped it to the floor. "I think my cleaning woman did a nice job, don't you?"

"Looks good to me. Everything I can see of it, that is. The light is a trifle dim in here." In fact it was as black as a whore's heart. But not nearly so cold. Congdon coughed. "So why'd you ask me here, Custis? Not for dinner, I'm thinking."

"I wanted t' ask you if you've heard anything about the movement of Chinese across the border lately."

"Are you still beating that dead horse, Custis? I already told you I don't know of anything. Still don't."

"A boy can always hope, eh?"

"How important is this anyway?"

Longarm shrugged, ignoring the fact that Dan couldn't see him. "I wish I could tell you, Danny. Congress wants t' know. Which is pretty much all I been told about it. The thing is, with them being involved it could mean this is important as all billy hell or just that they got their thumbs up their asses again."

"Well since we spoke the other day," Congdon said, "I did some looking around. Which you no doubt fully expected me to."

"Aye," Longarm said. "I was hopin'."

"I have to tell you again, Custis, the only Chinese I know anything about in our district are a few laundrymen and some cooks. I haven't heard anything about anyone using Chinese laborers. Or needing any. Don't forget, old son, this is the Texas border country. If we want cheap labor all we have to do is to hire some Mex workers. They'll work as cheap as any Chinaman and without causing any legal problems."

Longarm grunted. "I can't say as I understand it," he admitted.

"Hell, deputy, you don't have to understand anything. Just talk tough and pay whenever it's your turn to buy the beer."

"I just *knew* there would be a trick to this law shit," Longarm said with a laugh.

"Look, I don't want to rush you or anything, but I got a hot little number waiting with her pussy getting wet and I wanta be there when she fills it."

"Does your wife know anything about this?"

"Why, friend, she is the hot little number I mean."

"Then you'd best get back to her before she grabs a better man than you t' meet her needs. Wait a second here. I got another match. I'll light your way out."

"Thanks." Congdon hesitated. "No promises, but check with me again in a couple days, Custis. I'll keep my eyes open for stray Chinamen that aren't where they belong."

"Same place be all right?"

"Fine by me."

Longarm laughed. "For a puny-assed Texas Ranger, you aren't entirely useless, Danny."

"Until then."

Longarm waited until he heard Dan rise, then stuck his match to guide the ranger out of the sty and into the night.

Chapter 24

"Nathan dear, you please me like no one else ever has. Or ever could." Bobbi leaned across Longarm to set a cup of steaming coffee on the chairside table at his side, her free hand resting on the back of his head and lightly ruffling his hair.

Longarm wrapped his arm around Bobbi's impossibly thin waist. He tugged her shirttail out of her skirt and lifted it high, then placed his hand between her shoulder blades and pulled her closer, positioning her so he could suck and lightly nibble her left nipple. The girl began to tremble and after a few moments came to a shuddering climax. Lordy, she was easy to bring off. He gave her tit one final swipe of his tongue and said, "What time tomorrow will Bob be home?"

"Sometime in the afternoon," she said.

Longarm picked up the coffee cup, took a moment to smell the rich aroma coming off the dark surface, and took a sip. The coffee tasted even better than it smelled.

"Could I ask you something, Nathan?"

"Sure."

"Would you be embarrassed . . . that is, would you be ashamed . . . for Robert to know that I've fallen in love with you and that you, you know . . . I guess what I mean is, would you like to move into my room with me? It would save you the cost of that hotel room that you aren't ever in."

"Your brother wouldn't mind?"

"Robert wants me to be happy when it comes to those things. He puts up with me when I'm with men that he despises, so how much better would it be for me to sleep with someone that he actually likes?" She giggled. "For a change."

"Let me think about it."

"While you're thinking . . ." Bobbi dropped to her knees and began undoing the buttons at his fly.

"Whoa. None of that now."

"You don't want me to suck you?"

"I do but not right now. I wanta drink this coffee, then I gotta go see a man about a horse."

"I don't understand. What horse?"

"It's just an expression. Just means I got stuff I got t' do."

"But I thought . . . it's such a perfect afternoon to lie in bed and fuck."

"I agree. It would be. But first I got t' do this other stuff. I'll be back later."

"Can I come with you?"

"No," he said firmly. He lightly stroked Bobbi's cheek and cupped the back of her neck. She rolled her head back and closed her eyes. With his other hand Longarm lifted the coffee cup and took another drink.

"You are a wonderful man, Nathan James," Bobbi whispered.

"Button me up again, girl. I can't be goin' down the street with my dick hanging out."

She laughed. But did what he asked.

Longarm took one last swallow of the coffee—it really was very good—then stood. He was due to call at the telegraph office to see if there were any messages from Billy Vail.

Chapter 25

The message from Henry read: INFO SHIPMENT ARRIVING YOUR LOCATION FRIDAY RENDEV BULL TRAIN 6 MI SOU BRIDGE IN DARK OF MOON STOP INTERCEPT AND DETER STOP DETAIN LOCALS COMMA REJECT CHINESE ENTRY STOP

Henry said nothing about where this information came from but he obviously accepted it. And orders are orders. Longarm sent a return message acknowledging receipt of the instruction and destroyed the telegram in his hand after reading over the contents again.

Apparently, at least according to this, a shipment of Chinese was to cross the river Friday night to rendezvous with a bull train on the U.S. side. Longarm was to intercept them, send the Chinese back across the border, and arrest the men who were herding them. He would have thought it more sensible to identify who the workers were and then follow them to find their bosses. But then . . . orders were orders. If some idiot senator wanted to blow the investigation just to arrest a few low-level employees instead of shooting for the ringleaders, well, that was what would be done.

Probably, Longarm thought, the man who gave these orders wanted to generate some publicity for himself regarding the human smuggling ring.

And, damnit, orders are orders.

Longarm scowled as he tugged a cheroot out of his pocket, nipped off the twist, and spat it into the street before he struck a match and lighted his smoke.

It occurred to him that he was still under orders to keep his identity as a deputy marshal secret. Hell, he was not even supposed to be carrying his badge this time out. So how was he supposed to arrest the bullwhackers when he had no visible authority to do so?

Longarm thought about the problem for a minute or so, then turned and headed for the livery stable he had noticed two blocks over.

The place was small but he liked the looks of it. The barn had been painted not too long ago. The hay in the bunks was bright and clean, and the straw looked to be clean as well. The inside stalls had been freshly mucked out, and the tools of a hostler's trade were hung on the walls on racks or pegs as need be.

"The way you're looking me over," a voice came from the tack room, "a man would think you're wanting to buy the place. Want to make me an offer? Don't be shy now. Speak right up."

Longarm turned to see a slender, middle-aged man with a graying mustache emerge from the room full of saddles and harness. He stepped down onto the barn floor and carefully secured the door behind him before approaching Longarm.

"Nathan James," Longarm said with an outstretched hand.

"I'm Howard Tate," the liveryman said. His handshake was firm and his smile welcoming. "What can I do for you, Mr. James?"

"I need to hire a saddle horse if you have a good one. Something steady. I'll need it Friday afternoon and on, oh, maybe through to Saturday. Is that possible?"

"Of course it is. Uh, how good a rider are you?"

"Only middlin'," Longarm lied. He could handle pretty much anything that came under his saddle, but if he was going to be involved in an arrest he did not have to be wondering about the animal he was riding at the time. "Like I said, I'll be wanting something calm an' steady."

"I have something that should work for you. It's got some age on it, but it's sound and won't spook. I bought it off the army as surplus when they moved B Troop over to Fort Davis."

Longarm liked the sound of that. The horse had likely learned to stand steady despite the sound of gunfire. "Do you have one of those army saddles to go with him?"

"No saddle of your own, eh?"

"No, sir," Longarm agreed.

"That's no problem. I'll throw in a McClellan. Overnight, you say?"

Longarm nodded.

"Five dollars for the full weekend," Tate said. "Bring him back anytime Sunday. And, no offense, but since I don't know you I'll want a deposit up front. I'll return whatever is over your bill when we settle up. Twenty-five dollars should cover it."

Should cover every cent Tate had in the horse and tack both, but that was fair enough. Like the man said, he did not know this person who claimed to be Nathan James. "Do you want me to pay you now?" Longarm asked.

"When you pick him up will be soon enough."

Longarm smiled and shook the man's hand again. "Thank you, Mr. Tate. I'll see you Friday, say, just after lunch."

"I'll have him ready for you."

Longarm left the livery and headed back down the street. He was looking for a kid who might be relied upon to deliver a note.

Chapter 26

A man does not smoke inside a barn or other such tinder-dry structure. Longarm knew that. But it was driving him crazy. He wanted in the worst way to light up and enjoy a cheroot, but he could not safely do it inside the abandoned sty and Dan was taking forever to respond to his request that they meet again.

He could go outside to smoke but that ran the risk of someone seeing a stranger nosing around where he did not belong and calling the El Paso police to investigate.

Damnit!

He settled for sticking a cheroot in his jaw and chewing on the bitter leaf. That was most decidedly *not* the same thing as lighting up.

After a wait that was long enough to severely try Longarm's patience, he heard a faint scraping outside the flimsy door. A moment later the door was pulled open and a voice softly called, "Custis?"

"Here, Danny. Give me a second, I'll strike a match."

Longarm reached into his vest pocket and extracted a lucifer. He used his thumbnail to snap it aflame. The Texas Ranger slipped inside and joined Longarm in the old sty. Longarm blew the flame out and cupped the spent match in his palm until it was cold, then dropped it onto the straw-littered floor.

"Hope I didn't put you out none," Longarm said.

"Custis, if you knew what you'd interrupted you'd be plumb ashamed of yourself."

"Business?"

Congdon hesitated, then chuckled. "Pleasure."

"Oh. I apologize. I don't mind dragging a man out of business doin's, but I'm purely sorry to hear I took you away from . . . um . . . whatever it was that I took you away from."

"I'll get over it," Congdon said. He laughed and added, "Now I just hope that she does."

"Careful there, Danny, lest you be tellin' me more than is good for me t' know."

"So what is it that you wanted me here for, Custis?"

"I got some information, Dan. Not sure just how reliable it is, but it seems t' come from a good source. I also got a plan 'bout what to do about it. Seein' as how I'm not supposed t' show myself as a deputy an' so far as anyone is t' know I got no authority here, well, that's where you come in."

"You're gonna set something up and use my badge to complete the job, is that it?"

"In a nutshell . . . yeah."

"All right, Custis. Tell me what you got in mind."

Longarm shifted his unlighted cheroot to the other side of his jaw, leaned forward, and began to speak.

Chapter 27

Longarm shifted the stub of a half-smoked cheroot to the other side of his mouth and turned the page of the newspaper in his lap. He read a brief article about the Spice Islands, laid his cheroot in the ashtray, and took a swallow of Bobbi's excellent coffee. He uncrossed his legs and looked up as Bobbi approached him with a plate of sweets. Pecan pralines, thought. They looked awfully tempting. And tasted even better.

"Girl, if you keep this up, I'm gonna get hog fat an' useless." But he took another.

She smiled, accepting his words as a compliment. "What can I do for you?"

Longarm playfully waggled an eyebrow and said, "Might could be we can think of somethin'. Have us a little private time before Bob gets home." He slipped his hand underneath the hem of her dress and ran his hand up her leg.

Bobbi shivered and for a moment captured his hand between her thighs, squeezing hard. But she said, "It's too late. He's out back in the shed putting his things away. He should be in here in a minute or two."

Longarm folded the newspaper and laid it aside, then

stood and bent to kiss the homely girl. "You're sure you don't mind Bob knowin' about us?"

"I'm proud you're with me, Nathan. Real proud. You're the finest man I've known . . . probably ever. The very finest."

He kissed her again and gave her a quick hug, then moved his coffee and newspaper and ashtray over to the end table beside the settee, vacating her brother's easy chair for his use as Bob Temple was the master of this house. He was seated there, legs crossed and coffee steaming, when Bob came in through the back door.

"'Lo, Bob. Have a good trip, did you?"

Temple shrugged and settled into his chair. "Coffee," he called loudly. Bobbi quickly answered by bringing her brother a heavy china mug of the brew.

"Are we on?" Temple asked.

"You mean your plan to, um, make a little money below the border?"

"Exactly. Have you thought it over?"

"Some. I'll want to get a look at things on the ground first."

"Then we'd best do it soon," Temple said. "I want to do it this weekend."

Longarm shook his head. "That ain't possible. I got some other stuff going then."

"I thought we were going partners," Temple said. He did not look happy.

"We are, but like I said, Bob, I got other things going, too. Something I can't invite you in on. Something that can't wait."

"Care to tell me what that would be?"

"No," Longarm said. "Sorry, but I don't."

Temple thought about that for a moment, then grunted. "All right. I can wait." He raised his voice again and growled, "Woman, I need you. I want a wash and a shave. And something clean to wear."

"Yes, dear." Bobbi disappeared into the back of the house.

"She tells me you're sleeping here now," Temple said. "In her room?"

"That's right."

"Well, she's done dumber things than that," the one-armed man said. "Mind if I look at that newspaper? I'd like to catch up on things while I been away."

Longarm handed the paper over, then went back to his coffee. It would soon be time for him to go pick up that horse from the livery.

Chapter 28

Longarm laid his fork down and pushed back from the table. He stood and said, "If you folks would excuse me, there's some things I got to do." He leaned down to kiss Bobbi, thanked her for lunch, and said, "I'm not sure how long I'll be. At least overnight and maybe a couple days. Take care o' your big brother while I'm gone." He winked at Bob over Bobbi's shoulder, then turned and reached for his hat.

It was a short walk to the livery stable. Howard Tate had the rental horse saddled and waiting for him. Like most cavalry mounts the horse was a dull brown with very little white showing. It had a pencil neck and shoulder blades set much too vertical for a comfortable gait, but it appeared to be sound.

Longarm checked its feet. The shoes were fairly new and set tight. "I'll hand you a poke of horseshoe nails if you like," Tate offered.

"That'd be fine," Longarm told him. "You might throw in a tack hammer, too, an' saddlebags to carry the stuff in. Just in case."

"I can do that. Wait here, Mr. James. I'll be right back with everything. And, um . . ."

Longarm smiled. "I haven't forgotten, Mr. Tate. Twenty-five dollars on deposit. I'll dig that out while you get the saddlebags."

The exchange was made in short order, and Longarm swung into the age-cracked and creaky army surplus McClellan. From the uncertain feel of it he suspected one side of the saddletree was cracked, but it would do.

"All right?" Tate asked.

Longarm nodded once and kneed the brown into an easy walk. It was still early afternoon with hours of daylight remaining, and he did not want to reach his destination too soon.

He made two stops along the way out of town, first at a general mercantile where he bought jerky and some dried peaches, next at a café where he bought a sack of biscuits and freshly cooked bacon. He tucked his purchases into Howard Tate's saddlebags and rode slowly south along the Rio Grande following the directions Dan Congdon had given him.

The ford where the illegal entrants could be expected to cross was well over the six miles Henry's telegram had suggested but Dan knew the spot.

Could be expected to cross *if* Henry's information was correct, Longarm reminded himself. There was a very good probability that he was going on a wild-goose chase when his personal preference would have been to stay in the house and fuck Bobbi. But orders are orders.

"Come along now, jughead. We got us a ways t' travel."

Chapter 29

It was still daylight when he arrived at the ford on the Rio Grande. Did it without getting lost. More than twice. Or maybe three times. Fortunately the brown was a patient old hack and was not nervous about going into water.

Longarm thought only fleetingly about leaving tracks in the mud on the Texas side, then realized that this would be a common enough crossing point. No one was apt to think it strange if there were tracks here.

Once he was sure he had the right place and could expect company sometime after dark, he pulled well back from the riverbank and found himself a spot where he could wait and watch.

In west Texas there is no such thing as actual shade, but Longarm did the best he could under the shade-and-sun-speckled cover of a large mesquite.

He pulled Mr. Tate's old McClellan, scraped the ground bare to make sure he would not be getting any mesquite thorns in the blanket and put both saddle and blanket down so the horse's sweat could dry.

He staked the horse, then busied himself by harvesting some of the dark brown mesquite beans to feed to the horse. It seemed to find the treat more than merely acceptable.

When he was done with that Longarm washed his hands
with sun-bleached dirt to rid them of horse slobber, wiped
his hands on the seat of his britches, and pulled his food out
of his saddlebags, then settled down to wait.

Sundown came and went. Longarm stood and moved
around a bit to keep his legs from cramping. He would have
killed for a cheroot but did not want to risk someone smell-
ing smoke where there were not supposed to be any people.
Again he settled for taking one out and chewing it. He
would smoke the damn thing sometime later.

If there was anyone nearby—and there was supposed to
be—he could not see or hear them. But then he hoped they
could not spot him, either.

He squatted over his heels, broke a stick off the mesquite and used it to doodle patterns in the dirt, craned his
neck back and examined the clouds—there were only two
and neither of them was anything to brag about—and listened to the desert quail whistle as sundown approached.

The birds and small animals would be coming down to
water now, emerging from wherever they hid during the
heat of the day.

Not only the birds and small animals, though. Longarm
moved back a pace or so to make way for a rattlesnake that
had come out of its den in search of supper. He left it alone,
and it returned the favor.

An hour or more after dark, with a sliver of moon hanging low in the sky, he heard the creak and rattle of a wagon
in motion and the sharp crack of blacksnake whips carrying
on the night air.

It seemed he had indeed come to the right spot.

Chapter 30

"Watch the off leader, Miguelito. He might get that leg over the traces. Prod him. That's right. Do it again. I think they might be thirsty. Get the pail and fetch some water from the river. Good." The bullwhacker's voice carried clear on the night air.

Longarm reminded himself to make as little noise as he could. Silently he lifted his saddle blanket and brushed it off, laid it onto the brown's skinny back, and ran his hand over it carefully to make sure there were no kinks or folds that would dig into the horse's flesh and cause galls.

He picked up the saddle next and set it in place atop the blanket before letting the stirrups down, careful to make no noise. Finally he tugged the cinch tight and buckled it.

Now all he needed to do was to . . . wait. Again.

For half an hour or more he listened to the bullwhacker complain to his swamper Miguelito about the poor quality of the beer in Del Norte, the price of whores on the El Paso side—"What the hell. Do they think being on that side o' the river makes them a better fuck or something?"—the amount of fodder the oxen consumed every day, and his boots, which were too tight since the last time he got them wet and let them dry out under his bed.

The grumbling only stopped when Miguelito spoke up for the first time. "Senor. They come."

"What? Where?"

Stupid damn question, Longarm thought. Where exactly did this asshole think they would be in order to come across the ford from the Mexican side?

"There, senor."

"Okay. Right. I see 'em now."

There was silence for a little while, then Longarm heard the sound of distant voices, some of them jabbering in sing-song Chinese. Yeah, this was the right place, all right.

The Chinese, he understood, would likely wade across the Rio Grande on foot—it would be waist deep or so at this point—and meet the bull train. From there they were to be carried in the high-side wagons and on to their next stop on the illicit journey north.

Except this trip Custis Long knew something that the scofflaw importers of illegal slave labor did not.

This trip was going to be considerably shortened.

A point that was emphasized by the dull boom of a gunshot and a loud shout. "Hold your places and nobody gets hurt. You. Not another step or you'll be arrested for illegal entry. Take those Chinks right back where you got them. You. And you. Bring that wagon along. It's being impounded by the sovereign state of Texas, and you two are under arrest. The judge will go over the charges with you at your arraignment. Hey! What did I tell you? Turn your sorry asses around and cross right back over into Mehico where you belong. Now then, does everybody know what to do? Good."

Longarm smiled. Judging from the sounds of horses and the rattle of tack there had to be at least four rangers making this stop.

My, it was nice when a plan worked out the way it was supposed to.

Chapter 31

The plan went to shit with a rattle of gunfire and the blossoming of bright yellow muzzle flashes. From the south side of the damned river.

Longarm heard shrieks of terror from the Chinese, most of whom were still in the water. One of the rangers—he hoped it was not Dan Congdon—shouted, "Help me, I'm hit."

In the dim starlight he saw Chinese begin to drop, shot down by their own escorts. Probably they had paid every cent they had or could borrow for those bastards to mule them across into the land of promise and now they were being murdered by their own helpers.

Longarm spurred the brown forward. Leaning low in the saddle he stopped behind the tall sides of the bull wagon where both the contingent of rangers and the bullwhackers were huddled.

One of the rangers—Longarm could not see who it was—lay on the ground beside the off rear wheel of the ponderous wagon. Another knelt beneath the wagon and fired round after round toward the Mexican side, cranking his Henry rifle as fast as he could spit the slugs out.

The shooters on the other side shifted their aim, firing

into the oxen instead of trying to hit the well-protected rangers.

One sharpshooter, who must have had eyes like a cat to be able to see so well in the dark, took a bead on the ranger under the wagon. It took two shot to nail the ranger and put him down.

"Damnit, we're sitting ducks here." Longarm thought that was Dan Congdon's voice, although he could not be sure.

Sweat beaded under the brow of Longarm's Stetson. It trickled down his face and neck, leaving a sticky feeling behind.

He was not accomplishing anything sitting back here behind the wagon. No one was. And unless *some*body did something the entire ranger patrol was likely to be wiped out.

"Fuck it," Longarm mumbled aloud.

He tied the ends of his reins together and dropped them on the brown's skinny neck, hoping the horse learned enough while in service to know what that meant.

Automatically, without conscious thought, he reached down for the butt of his Winchester, which he always carried in a scabbard slung beside his saddle.

Except . . . this was not his saddle. And his carbine was back in his rented room in Denver.

That did not make things better, but it certainly did make them simpler.

He picked the reins up again and drew his Colt.

Longarm gave a shout and jabbed the brown in the flanks with his spurs.

Chapter 32

The brown horse charged into the river without hesitation. A wall of cold spray rose up on both sides, obscuring Longarm's vision.

Not that he needed to see. The enemy was straight ahead.

The curtain of water spray lessened when the horse reached deeper water so that its chest pushed a wave before it as the plunging animal surged past the bodies of Chinese illegals, shot down by the very men who had been charged with guiding and protecting them. Longarm counted four—no, five—bodies floating in the water. Other Chinese were ahead of him, scrambling up the far bank where gunfire continued to flash and thunder.

Longarm rode bent low in the saddle so as to make less of a target of himself. His thighs clamped hard on the barrel of the brown. The horse tossed its head and he got a face full of rough mane.

He was almost to the south bank before he returned the smugglers' fire.

No one can claim to shoot accurately from the bank of a lunging horse, but Longarm knew the tricks of timing that let him come close to accuracy.

He waited, enduring the threat of the smugglers' gunfire,

until the brown neared the Mexican side of the ford, then he sat upright in the saddle, judged the timing of the brown's water-strangled leaps, and triggered a shot low underneath the spear of flame released when someone fired a rifle toward the north bank.

Longarm was rewarded with a scream of pain and three other gunshots. At least one of those slugs whined unpleasantly near his head. But a miss, no matter how close, draws no blood. Longarm thumbed the hammer of his Colt and threw another shot toward the smugglers.

He was fairly sure he hit no one with that slug, but it had one desirable effect, and that was to draw the smugglers' fire away from the rangers and onto the much more difficult moving target that was in front of them on a brown horse.

A laboring brown, Longarm noticed now.

He reined away from the Mexican side, turned in the saddle and threw two more shots as suppressing fire.

Only one rifle answered as Longarm headed back toward U.S. soil.

He turned the other way and tried to take aim at that shooter, but suddenly the brown lost its footing and went down in the middle of the Rio Grande.

The horse threw its head and coughed, then rolled onto its side and went under.

Icy cold water closed over Longarm's head.

He tried to kick free of the saddle but his spur hung up in the stirrup.

The horse kicked and thrashed in its death throes, keeping Longarm from reaching down to his boot.

He had not had time to take a breath before going under the water. He opened his mouth reflexively and muddy water rushed in.

He had only seconds left to live.

Chapter 33

Longarm choked back an impulse to cough. That would surely have finished him. He fought for control, then swallowed the cold, silt-laden river water to clear his throat. More water seeped into his nose and he forced himself to exhale some of his precious air in order to get rid of that.

He had an almost overwhelming desire to breathe, which would have filled his lungs with water. He fought back the panic that threatened to overwhelm him and forced himself to remain calm.

He had seconds to live. Now he had to use them. Wisely. Or die.

The dying horse continued to thrash in the water, pushing Longarm down as it did so, holding him firmly by the foot so that he could not escape.

Longarm kicked hard, planting his free foot on the brown's rump and pushing so that the stirrup that trapped him was pulled up toward the seat of the army surplus saddle.

He kicked again. Hard. And managed to lever himself high enough for his head to break the surface long enough for him to gulp in a deep breath. Then he went under again, but deliberately this time.

He doubled his body over and, holding his breath, reached down to feel the stirrup that trapped his boot.

The cavalry boot was turned sideways in the unyielding wood and steel stirrup. Longarm took hold of the stirrup to steady it, then twisted his foot. The boot slipped free and Longarm kicked away from the now-limp and apparently dead brown horse.

He was exhausted, as much by his fight against panic as by the actual physical exertions of the near drowning, so weary he could not swim. He rolled onto his back and floated, allowing the strong current of the great Rio Grande to carry him with it.

Chapter 34

Longarm grounded on . . . something. He did not know what, knew only that he had encountered something solid in the river or beside it. He neither knew nor cared where he was or how far downriver he might have drifted. He knew only that his limbs trembled with fatigue and with the aftermath of his near panic when he thought for sure he was drowning and gone.

His legs trembled and his lungs burned. His vision was blurred and his throat and nose hurt from the intrusion of river water and his frantic efforts to expel it.

With considerable effort Longarm rolled over onto his belly. He puked out what silted water remained in his gut, then bent his head and took more of the foul-tasting stuff in so he could rinse the taste of vomit out of his mouth.

Finally he raised his head and tried to look around.

He did not know how long he had been in the river, thought he might have been delirious part of that time, but it is close to dawn now. Off in the distance the sky was turning pale. The stars had dimmed until now most of them were gone. The air was cool, and Longarm shivered, as much from reaction as from the temperature. He coughed again and tried to struggle upright.

He could not. All he could manage was to drag himself forward until his head and shoulders rested on rocky but blessedly dry soil.

With his legs and lower body bobbing in the current of the Rio Grande, Custis Long closed his eyes and went gratefully into a healing sleep.

Chapter 35

He heard something. A scuffling in the gritty sand of the riverbank, perhaps. Slowly he lifted one glued-shut eyelid. He saw a pair of feet, small and brown and muddy. Longarm rolled his head to the side and opened the other eye, fluttering the lid until he could see properly.

A small boy was standing beside his face. The kid wore a pair of many-times-patched trousers. He was perhaps five years old. When the boy saw Longarm looking at him he spun around in fright, screamed, "Mama," and ran away shouting.

Longarm was desperately weary and still somewhat confused after being tumbled about and rolled over and over in the waters of the Rio Grande. He tried to get up and did manage to lever his chest off the ground, but from the waist down he was still in the water. His legs were chilled to the point of no longer working, and his mind felt like his head was stuffed with cotton wool. There was a sour taste in his mouth and his head ached like the devil himself was trying to pound it apart. The hot sun seared his neck and back even while his legs felt half frozen from the immersion in the moving water. What with one thing and another, Custis Long felt like shit.

Piss on it. Longarm dropped his face to the gravel and once again drifted away.

The next time he opened his eyes he was surrounded. Sort of, anyway.

The same little boy was there. So was an older and slightly larger version, similar right down to the bare feet and ragged pants. Along with them was a chubby woman with very dark skin and long, shiny black hair. She too wore the patched white canvas trousers but she added a beaded Mexican-style top to her ensemble. Longarm guessed her age to be somewhere in her forties. She could have been the mother or the grandmother of the boys. Either would have worked.

The boys were jabbering in Spanish. Their mother spoke to them and they obediently jumped to comply. The older of the two took one of Longarm's arms. The younger stepped into the river and tried to wrestle Longarm's legs out of the water. The stocky woman took his other arm. Together on her command they all began to pull.

Slowly they dragged Longarm out of the swirling waters of the Rio Grande and onto dry land. They continued dragging him, bumping painfully over small rocks and the occasional goathead or button cactus.

He could not begin to estimate how far they took him like that, all of them straining and puffing from the exertion. He knew that it felt like they carried him for miles even though common sense ruled that out.

Dry dust invaded his nose. Sharp pains raked his knees and belly. The journey never seemed to end. Then suddenly he felt the cool of shade pass overhead.

His benefactors turned him over onto his back. It appeared he was on the porch or veranda of an adobe house.

The woman and little boys strained some more and managed to half lift, half roll their nearly inert guest onto a low-slung hammock that was suspended from some of the support poles that held up the loosely piled brush roof.

The woman lifted Longarm's head and pushed a corn shuck–stuffed canvas pillow behind his neck.

She smiled and said something that he did not understand. Then she patted him and brushed her hand gently over his cheeks. She spoke some more. The only word he really grasped was "*Dios.*" Which was just fine by him. He reckoned he needed God's help plenty right now.

Longarm closed his eyes and once again drifted away.

Chapter 36

When Longarm woke up his head was fuzzy and his chest aching. He fought back an impulse to puke, then tried to sit up. The bobbing, bouncing support of the hammock did not help. Had he been prone to seasickness he would have lost his last three days of meals. Once he did manage to get more or less into a sitting position he discovered two things. He was covered with a light blanket that slipped down to his waist. And he was bare-assed naked beneath the blanket.

He shook his head to try to clear it, but that only started a pounding headache. He tried to judge how long he had been out but he could not.

Over on one side of the portal the older of the children was diligently pouring sand into Longarm's boots. It took him a moment to understand why, but the reason was to dry the boots without applying any sort of direct heat that would crack and quite possibly shrink the leather.

On a clothesline suspended from a roof support to a stout cactus he recognized the articles of clothing hanging there. Which explained how he came to be naked. Apparently the chubby woman not only hung his clothes, she washed them first.

His gun belt dangled from the ceiling, and his Colt .45

lay on a table close to hand. It was pointed away from him so he could not see into the cylinder chambers, but he would have to assume that the revolver was still empty after his assault on the smugglers. He would have to correct that as soon as possible.

But not—he yawned—not now.

Custis Long lay back, stretched, and pulled the blanket high under his chin.

What he needed now was sleep. Healing, blessed sleep.

He woke the second time to the feel of a hand on his dick. Stroking, kneading, encouraging the erection that soon grew.

Longarm opened his eyes to see the face of the fat Mexican woman. She smiled, continuing to stroke him, and by gesture indicated that if he wanted to fuck or perhaps only a blow job she would be glad to offer those services. *"Un' peso,"* she said, holding up a finger to indicate what her fee would be.

He blanched and shook his head. Even if he had been feeling good, which he most assuredly was not, he would not have been interested in cutting a slice of this.

"No, ma'am. Thank you, but no."

"Un'?"

Longarm shook his head again. Hell, he wondered if he had any money to pay her with anyway. He had been out so hard she and her boys were able to strip his clothing off. They could have pilfered any amount they pleased while he was out like that.

Yet when he tugged open the carefully tied scrap of waste cloth that was sitting on the table beside his revolver, his money was there. As far as he could tell there was not a red cent missing.

"Un' peso," she said again.

"Agua," Longarm responded. *"Agua, por favor."*

The woman bobbed her head and barked out something. The smaller of the boys went running to get Longarm some

water. He was mighty pleased to see that the boy fetched it
from a bucket and not that damned river. He had drunk quite
enough of that already.

The boy gave him a drink and the woman brought a plate
of beans. Which was no doubt all she had to offer.

"My clothes," he said, indicating with his hands. "Are
they dry yet?" The fabric items had been drying in the sun
for . . . who knew how long, while his leather gear was dried
in the shade.

Once Longarm made it clear what he wanted, the older
boy brought his things while the younger, under his mother's
direction, poured the now-cold sand out of Longarm's boots
and carefully wiped the insides before returning them to their
owner.

It felt good to be dressed again. Made him feel damn near
human.

"Gracias," he said. *"Muchas gracias."*

The woman and the boys chattered at him but he had no
idea what they were saying. Whatever it was, he was deeply
in their debt. He picked up his Colt and gun belt and carefully refilled the chambers with the spare cartridges that
had been in his pocket. Once the gun belt and revolver were
properly situated, Longarm felt whole again. He dropped
some of his coins into his pockets but held out five gleam-
ing yellow double eagles. Those would spend as easily below the border as it would across the river in Texas. Gold is
accepted pretty much everywhere.

The woman raised her chin but offered no protestations
against taking the money. He gathered that she was quite
desperately poor. A hundred dollars U.S. was bound to help.
And what she and her boys had done for him was damned
sure worth that.

"Gracias," he said again, then turned away, heading up-
stream on the Mexican side of the river. He did not want to
risk going under that water again. Better to hike this side

until he reached the ford where the Chinese had crossed earlier.

And once he got across he could walk back to El Paso in the cool of the approaching night.

Lordy but he did still feel shaky after his near drowning.

Chapter 37

He found the ford easily enough. By the dead Chinese lying about on the ground there. He supposed the ones who died in the water floated away. Just like he might have but for a bit of luck.

The smugglers, damn them, must have slaughtered the remaining Chinese lest the poor sons of bitches bring the authorities down on them.

Longarm waded into the river once more. He scowled when the water ran over the tops of his cavalry boots and chilled his feet and lower legs again. Walking in wet boots was apt to cause blisters. Walking in his bare feet in dry and thorny country like this would cause worse than a few blisters. He had no choice but to climb out of the water and hike upriver on the U.S. side now.

The road, such as it was, was fairly clear and easy to follow. Trudging along at a steady three to four miles an hour Longarm made the outskirts of El Paso some time in the wee hours of the morning and tapped on Bobbi's windowpane shortly before dawn flooded the streets with light.

"Oh, my God, what happened to you?" she cried when she saw him. "Where's your hat? Why do you look so bedraggled?"

"It's a long story. Can I come in?" he asked.

"You know you can. Go to the back door. I'll unbolt it for you."

Longarm climbed wearily onto the porch, stumbled over a washtub Bobbi had left there, and pulled the back door open. Bobbi was there, wearing only a thin chemise. She clutched him close and for a while there he thought she might never stop hugging him.

"I worried about you, dearest," she blubbered, wiping her nose on his shirt.

"Hey, I said I'd come back, didn't I?" He smiled and bent to kiss the skinny young woman.

"I'm so glad you did. I don't know what I would ever do without you, Nathan. You are my one true love."

"Bobbi, honey, there's somethin' you got t' understand . . ."

"Shush, darling," she said, laying a finger over his lips to silence him. "I know you aren't mine forever. But in my heart you will be. When it's time for you to go, well, do what you have to do. I will remember you and love you always." She managed a crooked smile. "No matter how many bums I take to bed."

He kissed her again. "Fair enough. Now would you mind if I get some sleep, please. I've had a, um, strenuous time lately."

She took him into her bedroom, helped him off with his clothes, and tucked him under the sheets. "I have to go fix breakfast for Robert now, but I'll be back as soon as he's settled at the table."

Longarm barely heard. He was already slipping into a deep and healing sleep.

Chapter 38

He woke slowly, feeling like he was surrounded by warm . . .
Longarm's eyes snapped open. Fact is, he *was* surrounded by
warmth. Wet warmth. As in the oft-enjoyed and very fondly
remembered feel of his erect dick being deep inside a
woman's mouth.

He looked down to see the back of Bobbi's head moving
gently up and down. Longarm laughed. And closed his eyes
again, giving himself up to the delightful sensations.

The feelings built, forming deep in his groin and flood-
ing out of his balls and into Bobbi's warm and receptive
mouth. She gagged once on the flow of his juice but continued to suck until she had all of it, then she sat up with
a coquettish smile, and with Longarm watching, swallowed
what he had just given her.

"Helluva nice way t' wake up," he said. Bobbi laughed
and wiped her mouth, then produced a hand towel and carefully dried his cock and balls.

"What time is it?" he asked.

"About noon. I have your lunch on the table."

"Shit. I shouldn't'of slept s' long. I got to go."

"Nathan! You have to eat, you know."

"Later."

"Can't I make you a sandwich then? Something you could take with you?"

"All right. If you can do it quick while I get dressed."

"I'll have it ready for you by the time you get your boots on, dear."

The girl was as good as her word. When Longarm emerged from the bedroom they shared she handed him a slice of buttered bread folded over with a chunk of fatty bacon wrapped inside.

"Perfect," he said. "Thanks." He bent and quickly kissed the girl good-bye, then headed out the front door of the Temple house.

If he remembered correctly, this was Sunday afternoon, and he had to find Ranger Dan Congdon before it was too late to put his plan in motion.

Chapter 39

He hated to do it, but on a Sunday afternoon he had no idea where in hell to look for Dan. The only logical thing he could think of was to take his chances on being recognized and go straight into the lion's den; he headed for the El Paso ranger headquarters.

A skinny fellow with a drooping mustache bigger than he was was seated at the sergeant's desk in the lobby. Fortunately he was not one of the Texas Rangers whom Longarm had encountered before.

"Can I help you, mister?"

"Could be. I'm looking for a ranger o' yours. Name of Dan Congdon."

"What is the nature of your business with Ranger Congdon?"

"That's personal an' private," Longarm said. "I'm sorry, but it's not somethin' I'd feel free t' discuss with anybody else."

"And you are . . . ?"

"Nathan James, sir."

"Ranger Congdon knows you, does he?"

"Yes, sir. He . . . truth is, Sergeant, he ran me in for drunk an' disorderly last week. But he was straight with me. Handled things like a professional, if you know what I mean. I admired him for that. Now I got some information that he oughta have."

"Ranger Congdon is not on duty at this time, but I suppose I could send a boy to fetch him. Do you want to wait here?"

"If it's all the same t' you, Sergeant, standin' here in your ranger headquarters makes me kinda nervous. Have the boy tell Ranger Congdon t' meet me in that same saloon where he arrested me. Could you do that?"

"I suppose so." The skinny ranger leaned forward and eyed Longarm with obvious suspicion.

"I'd be happy t' pay for the kid t' deliver that message." Longarm reached into his pocket and pulled out a quarter, which was the smallest coin he happened to have on him at the moment.

"All right. You go on to wherever that was. I'll get your message to the ranger. Mind you now, it's up to him whether he wants to show up or not."

"Yes, sir. Thank you."

Longarm headed down the street, took one wrong turn, and eventually ended up at the Topeka Saloon. The same fellow was wearing the apron today. Norm? No, Longarm recalled, it was Herm. Herm Johnson. Longarm took a pickled sausage and a chunk of cheese from the free lunch spread and ordered a beer. He used his mustache to strain the head off his beer and took a long, satisfying swallow. He was about to drink again when a kid came in carrying a newspaper bag over his shoulder.

"Extra, extra, read all about it. Shoot-out with smugglers south of the city. United States marshal killed. Rangers' lives spared by heroic action. Read all about it."

"I'll take one o' those, son." Longarm plucked a dime out of the change he had gotten for his beer and handed it to the boy in exchange for one of the single-sheet extras of the *El Paso Intelligencer*.

Who the hell else could have been working El Paso last Friday night? Whoever it was, Longarm figured he very likely knew the poor son of a bitch who got caught in that fusillade of bullets.

He set his free lunch down on a napkin, wiped his mouth, and took one look at the headlines.

He blanched a pale, pasty white as soon as he did so.

"U.S. Marshal Custis Long Dies." And a subhead read, "Killed Saving the Lives of Four Texas Rangers."

"Jesus!" Longarm blurted.

Chapter 40

Longarm was only halfway through the article, wondering where the hell the fellow who wrote the story got his so-called facts, when out of the corner of his eye he saw a tall, lanky fellow wearing a revolver on his belly and a cut-down shotgun on his side. The man's hat was a battered old Kossuth that came down over his ears. His coat, black as was the hat, was buttoned all the way to his chin.

The newcomer went from patron to patron, whispered something to each man and passed along to the next. Shortly after he spoke to them the other gents drained off their beers and ambled slowly out of the Topeka. Too slowly by half, Longarm thought. Something was up here.

Longarm waited for the fellow—a preacher, maybe—to come spread the word his way. Instead the man ordered a beer from Herm Johnson, paid for it, and slid down the bar close to where Longarm stood. While he was doing that, Herm sidled out the back door.

That left just two people in the place, Longarm and this fellow in the ill-fitting hat.

"Mr. James?"

"That's right. I'm Nathan James."

"It's a pleasure to meet you, Mr. James." The fellow's face

split, his lips thin and his smile unconvincing. He stuck his hand forward.

Longarm had a feeling it would not necessarily be a smart thing for him to give this gent his gun hand. Instead he coughed into his fist. When his hand came down it rested on the age-worn butt of his Colt.

The man saw and backed away. But he did not lift his own hands away from his guns.

"We don't want to have trouble now, do we, Mr. James?"

"I'm just standin' here havin' a beer and waitin' for a friend. Is there something you have in mind?"

"You friend would like to meet you over at the ranger headquarters," the tall fellow said.

"Fuck you, mister. I don't know you nor don't want to."

The fellow unbuttoned the top two buttons of his coat and began to reach inside. He found himself with the muzzle of a Colt revolver beneath his nose.

"Be good if you keep your hands where I can see them," Longarm drawled.

"I . . . no harm intended, mister. I'm just reaching for a badge."

"What kinda badge?"

"Texas Rangers."

"I'll consider that possibility later. Next question, friend, is how you happened t' spot me standin' here minding my own damn business."

A hint of smile flickered over the ranger's—if he indeed was a ranger—thin lips. "That's easy enough. It's because I drink here, too. Most of us rangers do. I recognize all the regular customers. You're the only one I didn't already know, at least good enough to know they belong."

Holding his hands well away from his sides, the ranger said, "My name is Matt Schrank. Yours?"

"Nathan James."

"No, you're not. Nathan James's real name is Custis Long. He died down along the Rio Grande two nights ago.

You probably read about it in the newspaper this afternoon. If you can read, that is."

"Look, Schrank, I'm not gonna stand here an' argue with an asshole like you. Where's Danny Congdon?"

"Dan and three other rangers are right outside that doorway. Well, some of them are. Some are out back in case you try to make a break in that direction."

"Call Danny in here."

"Why should I?"

"Oh, shit, I dunno. Maybe because while your gun is bigger'n mine, mine is right here in hand while yours is in the leather."

"I've heard worse arguments," Schrank said after taking a moment to ponder the matter. He turned and roared. "Congdon. Front and center."

The saloon batwings pushed open and Danny stepped inside. He was holding a Winchester leveled in the general direction of the barroom.

"Custis! *Jesus Christ.*" Dan lowered the barrel of his carbine and came rushing across the floor to Longarm.

Chapter 41

After about two minutes of back-pounding, hand-pumping pandemonium, the tall ranger who first braced Longarm ordered the front doors bolted.

Danny leaned close to Longarm and whispered, "Schrank is our sergeant. He's an awful good man."

The sergeant waited until the doors were locked and the assemblage of rangers, and one lone United States deputy marshal, were alone in Herm Johnson's saloon. Then he turned and leaned back with his elbows on the bar.

"Dan tells us you're here undercover. Would you mind telling us what that is about?"

Longarm shrugged. "Why it is that I can't reveal myself as a deputy, I got no idea. It don't make sense to me but some asshole clerk back in Washington City seemed t' think it was necessary. Personally I think it's stupid, but orders is orders, so for now I reckon I'm still Nathan James."

"Fair enough, but your Chinese smugglers seem to have been busted up now," Schrank said.

One of the other rangers—a youngster named Ted something, who looked to be about fifteen years old . . . and actually might have been because all the Texas Rangers required of a man was that he have grit and a good rifle—went around behind the bar and broke out a bottle and glasses for all.

"You boys nabbed the bullwhacker," Longarm said. "Him an' his swamper. What I'd like t' get is the fella that hired them. He's the one we want if we really want t' break this up."

"There were only two men on the Texas side of the river Friday night," Sergeant Schrank said. "We have both of them in custody."

"Do you really?" Longarm asked with a grin. "In the city jail, are they?"

"Yes, of course. We don't have our own lock-up facility."

"So Danny already demonstrated," Longarm said, his grin staying right where it was.

Longarm picked up his glass of whiskey—it was not rye but not entirely rotten stuff, either—and took a slow, contemplative drink. "Y'know, boys," he said, "that hard-ass Nathan James fella is already known in your jail over there. I'm thinking he should be put in irons an' dragged in all over again."

"Pardon me?"

"You heard me. Danny? You wanta do the honors again, pard?"

"Believe me, Custis, it will be a great pleasure for me to throw your ass in jail again."

"Then let me finish this here whiskey an' we can go get the ball rolling." He laughed. "Just don't forget t' come release me. Which reminds me . . . that judge? I'm thinking come Monday he should maybe have a toothache or somethin'. I might be needing more time behind bars than a Sunday afternoon incarceration would allow. Can you arrange that?"

Congdon turned to his sergeant for the answer. "Well?"

"Why, Mr. James, I think we can handle that for you.

How long do you think this toothache should keep the man incapacitated?"

"I'd hope a couple days should do it. It's worth that much time behind bars t' take the chance anyway."

The tall sergeant nodded. "Consider it done. Now Ranger Congdon, I'm ordering you to toss this miscreant into the pokey. Drink up, boys." Schrank tossed his own whiskey back, hitched up his britches, and headed for the front door along with the rest of the rangers, leaving only Dan Congdon behind to open the back door so Herm Johnson could get back into his own saloon.

Dan came back to the bar, winked at Longarm, then finished his own whiskey before pulling out his handcuffs and once again securing them onto Longarm's wrists.

"Don't forget t' pocket my revolver," Longarm cautioned.

"Yeah, I almost forgot. We ready?"

"Lead on, boss." Longarm meekly followed his captor to the city jail for booking.

Chapter 42

According to Sergeant Schrank the Anglo who was arrested Friday night was a beefy son of a bitch named Scott, the only name he gave when he was booked into the jail. He was wearing red long johns and bib overalls, and he was Custis Long's target for the next day or two.

"You again," the turnkey said with a scowl. The man was not privy to Longarm's little ploy and knew nothing of the real reason Longarm was here. "James, is it, smart-ass? Trying to be like your asshole cousins, eh. Well let me tell you, you ain't gonna like it in my jail. No special care. No special food. None of that shit."

"Fuck you," Longarm snarled.

The turnkey used his heavy ring of keys to slash Longarm across the back of his head then gave him a shove. Longarm went sprawling onto the seldom-cleaned floor, blood running from the split in his scalp caused by the blow.

Before Longarm could orient himself and turn around, possibly to retaliate, the turnkey slammed the heavily barred iron door shut with a loud clang. He quickly locked the door and then, safe behind it, taunted Longarm with a smirk.

If Longarm's look could have killed, that bastard would have been dead on the floor outside the big holding cell.

That was something that grieved Custis Long. As much as he believed in law, and as much as he took pride in serving it, there was something about it that drew pricks and bullies into it. With badges and even more so running prisons and jails. Turnkeys were too often vicious sons of bitches who preyed on men who could not fight back.

Not that there was anything Longarm could do about this one. At least not right now. And in fact he may well have done Longarm a favor by this.

Longarm came shakily to his feet and tried to stanch the flow of blood that was running down the back of his neck and soaking into his shirt. He had no kerchief—the had taken that away from him on the theory that it could be used to hang himself or to strangle someone else—so all he could do was to pulled his shirttail out of his trousers and lift the already bloody shirt high. He pressed the cloth tight against the break in his scalp and eventually thought the bloody cut clotted over. He carefully took the cloth away and turned his back to the man seated next to him.

"Tell me, neighbor, is that son of a bitch still bleedin'?" The man he just happened to be sitting next to was the burly fellow who called himself Scott. He was wearing bib overalls and red long johns, and he was the link in the smuggling chain who had been arrested on Friday night.

"Let me take a look." Scott seemed friendly enough. He leaned close and pushed Longarm's matted hair aside until he could see the jagged split in his scalp. "It looks like shit and you ain't gonna be able to wear a hat for a spell, but at least it's stopped bleedin'."

Longarm turned to face him and Scott extended his hand. "I'm Jake," he said. "Jake Scott."

"I'm Nathan James," Longarm told Jake Scott. "No relation to them famous Jameses though, at least not that my mama ever said."

Scott shook Longarm's hand with a firm and friendly grip. "What are you in here for, Nathan?"

Longarm grinned at him. "Oh, maybe a little bit disorderly. They said I'm drunk, too, but you can see for yourself that I ain't. Bastards lie, you know. How's about you?"

"Smuggling. But I'll be outta here soon as I see the magistrate. They got no proof of anything."

"Reckon we're both stuck here till tomorrow morning then," Longarm said. "Got any cards for a little gin rummy or somethin' to pass the time 'til then?"

"You're kidding, right? I mean, they take all the stuff like that before they toss a body in here."

"Yeah, Jake, I'm kidding. Wish I wasn't, but I am. So tell me about this smuggling shit. I'd think it would be dead easy around here. Just cross the river an' there you be."

"You really want to hear?"

"As a matter of fact, Jake, I do want to hear. The thing is, I'm looking for a new racket. Lookin' for a way to make a little coin, if you know what I mean. D'you think there might be a future in this smuggling racket of yours? If other fellas can come in on it, that is. I wouldn't want t' horn in on anything you're doing."

"Yeah, I could tell you a little about it." Jake smiled. "If you got time to listen."

Longarm laughed. "Now who's being the smart-ass. But yeah, Jake, I'd be real interested in learning about this deal."

"Then sit back and listen, Nathan, and . . . say, I just had a thought."

"What's that, Jake?"

"If you can drive a bull team . . . can you?"

"I have before. I'd want t' get to know my oxen, o' course, but yes, I can drive 'em."

"The fella I work for is always looking for reliable people. Men he can count on. You know?"

"Uh-huh."

"I might . . . no guarantees, mind you, but I might be able to put you and him together. See if you like each other."

"Tell me more about him if you don't mind. I'd want t' make sure I make a good impression on him."

Oh, Longarm was *definitely* interested now.

Chapter 43

Once they were freed from the confining bars of the El Paso city jail two days later, Jake helpfully showed Longarm to a barber-surgeon's shop where he trusted the barber. "Can you believe it? The man actually washes his hands *every* time before he works on somebody."

"Meticulous fella, huh?" Longarm said.

"And then some. But he's good. You won't hardly feel a thing."

That was not entirely accurate. The needle piercing the tough meat of his scalp and crisscrossing back and forth with light cotton thread hurt like a son of a bitch. But Longarm had felt worse. And if he lived long enough would feel worse than this again, he was sure. He had a slug of whiskey—or two—to help contain the pain and sat still while the barber did his work.

"There," the man said once he was satisfied. He stood back for a moment to admire his handiwork. "Now a shave and a bath?"

"Lordy, right now I'd kill for a bath."

The barber gave him an odd, half-frightened look.

"It's just a, uh, figure o' speech. I'm not interested in killin' nobody right now."

"You from someplace else?" Longarm asked.

"Aye, isn't everybody." The barber offered no details and Longarm knew enough to not ask.

"Shave first, then the bath?" Longarm asked.

"Aye, I think so."

The man had a delicate, feathery touch with a razor blade and Longarm felt about halfway human once he was done with the shave. He made it the rest of the way back to human after a refreshing bath. There was even a pretty little Chinese girl in the bathing room to scrub his back and, very gently, wash the blood out of his hair. He suspected she might be available for other services too but did not pursue that line of thought; he had his own lined up back at the Temple house.

After bathing he had no desire to put the bloody shirt back on. Instead he carried it out of the barbershop and wore only his vest outside.

"I got t' make a stop, Jake. Get me a decent shirt that ain't all stiff with dried blood two days old. Come along with me an' meet the friends I'm stayin' with."

"Sure. There's no hurry."

Longarm led the way, and they walked out to the street where Bob and Bobbi lived.

"These are good folks, mind. I'm thinkin' you'll like them."

"And friend of yours." Jake smiled. "And all that crap."

Longarm let himself inside the gate and mounted the Temple porch, motioning Jake to join him.

Bobbi came rushing out and threw herself onto Longarm's chest. "Nathan. I was so worried about you. I'm so glad you're home safe and sound."

"I'm fine, darlin'." He laughed. "Just got tossed in the pokey for a couple days. Truth is, I'm surprised I didn't run inta Bob there, too."

"He's been working. He got a job making some short hauls across the New Mexico line and back. He should be home again tonight. Come in, please. Can I bring you a drink? How about you, sir?"

"Bobbi, this here is my friend Jake Scott. Jake, Miss Roberta Temple."

Jake whipped his hat off and bowed. "My pleasure, miss."

"Please come in out of the heat. Both of you."

Bobbi stood aside and held the door for the two men to enter, then she scurried into the kitchen and quickly returned with a bottle of rye whiskey—there had been none in the house before but Longarm had mentioned a liking for the Maryland distilled rye—two glasses, and a pitcher of water.

"If there is anything else I can get you . . ."

Longarm winked at her and whispered. "There will be. Later."

Bobbi blushed and pretended to be highly offended. But he could see that the girl was pleased.

"Are you hungry? I'll start fixing your lunch," she said without waiting for an answer, then she whisked out of the parlor and into the kitchen that was her own domain.

Chapter 44

That afternoon Longarm and Jake were still relaxing with a
pail of beer that Bobbi fetched from somewhere nearby
when Bob got in. Bobbi helped him wash up—apparently it
was the shits trying to properly wash with only one hand—
then he joined the other two men in the parlor.

"Jake an' I might have something going, Bob. Might take
me away for a few days. Maybe a few weeks actually."

Bob's displeasure at that news showed clearly in his expression. "I thought you and me had something going, too."

"That's right, my friend, but it has occurred to me that
Jake might be a good man for the deal you have in mind. It
never has appealed all that much to me, if you want t' know
the truth. I'm shy about goings-on on t'other side o' the
border. Never mind why but the reasons are pretty powerful." Longarm suggested just how powerful they might be
by wrapping both hands around his throat. As if a hang-
man's noose.

"That's why you been slow to get going?"

"'Tis, Bob. But I'm thinking you an' Jake both have the
same, um, outlook on things. He might be just the fella you
been needing."

"Gentlemen," Jake said, "I'm sitting here fat and ignorant

while you two talk about me. What the hell is it you have in mind?"

"It's Bob's idea. He'll have t' be the one to tell you about it, Jake. If he wants to, that is. This is strictly his deal an' I wouldn't undercut him on it."

"I don't know Jake all that well," Bob said. "No offense, you understand."

"None taken," Jake said. He retreated into his mug of cool, crisp beer.

"You didn't know me all that well, neither, Bob. Hell, for all you knew at the time I coulda been a ranger or a deputy something or other. But we got t' know each other and you trusted me. Why, you even encouraged me t' take your own sister for my girlfriend. Now that I've spent a little time in the jail with Jake here I'm thinking he could be just the man t' help you with your plan."

"What sort of plan is that?" Jake asked.

Bob looked uneasily toward Longarm for reassurance, then said, "It's a breaking and entering. So to speak. It wouldn't violate any American laws 'cause the place I have in mind—never mind exactly where that is, at least not until I'm comfortable with you—is down the other side of the river."

Jake thought for a moment and took another pull at his beer, then turned the mug up and emptied it. "I been known to bend the law a time or two."

"Anything serious?" Bob asked.

Jake grinned. "Not to me it wasn't."

That got a laugh out of Bob. He chuckled a little, then turned and roared, "Woman, we need another pail of beer."

"Two," Longarm amended. "I'm paying."

"Hell, if you're paying, make it three." Bob laughed.

Bobbi collected the two pails they had already emptied and took them away to exchange them for three full ones. Longarm slipped her a ten-dollar gold piece to pay for their evening of drinking.

By the time the mantel clock chimed eleven, Bob Temple and Jake Scott were well on their way to becoming asshole buddies. They were deep in discussion about how best to take the Mexican bank Bob had in mind as a target.

At least that problem was solved, Longarm told himself as he climbed a trifle unsteadily to his feet. "Time for this ol' boy to go to bed," he said.

"I expect we'd best crawl in our own selves," Bob said. He turned his head and shouted, "Woman, come lay out blankets and a pillow on the couch for my friend Jake here. He'll be staying with us for a spell."

Bobbi did not seem at all put out by the instruction. She hurried to lay out blankets, a sheet, and a down-filled pillow for their guest.

"I'll go on back," Longarm said. He gave Bobbi's elbow a squeeze. "Don't be far behind me, hear?"

She gave him an appreciative smile and continued on with her task.

Longarm walked back to the bedroom he was sharing with the girl, stripped, and crawled between the sheets. Bobbi, he hoped, would not be far behind.

Chapter 45

"Oh. Ah, ah. Yes. Yessssss. Harder, baby, deeper. Yes!" Bobbi drove her little ass up, down, and sideways, pumping as hard and as steadily as a steam engine driving a piston. All Longarm had to do was to hang on and enjoy the ride.

He pounded the girl's belly until he thought he was surely hurting her and she cried out for more. If she kept this up she just might break something. The bed if not a bone.

"Yes, yes, sweetie, harder."

If that was what she wanted . . . Hell, he thought about strapping his spurs on so he could hang on tighter.

Suddenly the door opened and the room was flooded with light. Bob stood there, a burning lamp in his hand.

"Keep it down, you two. You're going to give us a bad name with the neighbors if you don't shut up," he growled. Then he withdrew, taking the light with him and pulling the door closed behind him.

It was a good thing Bob Temple didn't mind who fucked his sister. It would ruin Longarm's whole day to get a bullet from an irate husband or father up his exposed ass.

Bobbi stopped banging her belly against Longarm's, looked with apparent horror toward the door . . . and then broke up with the giggles. "I'm sor . . . sor . . . sorry. Sort of." She clamped her hand over her mouth in a futile attempt to keep the giggling at bay.

Longarm could feel her belly ripple and tremble against his as she laughed and that got him to laughing along with her. Within a minute or so both of them were howling with laughter and rolling back and forth on Bobbi's very rumpled and sweaty bed.

"Oh, oh. Did you hear? Oh!"

The bedroom door opened again and once more Bob stood there with his lamp in hand. "Now what has you two going on so?"

"We . . . we . . . oh."

"What she's tryin' to tell you is that . . ." Longarm paused, scratched his nuts, and said, "Shit, Bob, I dunno what she's tryin' to say. But she sure as shit is funny when she says it."

"Are you two having fun?"

"Matter o' fact we are."

"Thirsty?"

"Uh-huh."

"There's a little beer left in this pail," he said. He set the lamp down on Bobbi's nightstand, stepped back into his bedroom, and reappeared carrying a pail that was about half full of warm, almost flat beer.

Bob perched on the side of Bobbi's bed, completely unmindful of the fact that both his sister and his friend were naked as jaybirds. He used his one hand to deftly take a drink from the pail, then offered it first to Longarm and then to Bobbi.

"Damn, that's good," Longarm said, wiping his mouth with the back of his hand and smoothing his mustache.

"Could I ask you something, Nathan? Something that's been pestering me ever since I first thought about it?"

"Of course, Bob. Anything."

"When you strain beer through your mustache, does it taste like pussy all the time? Or just when the pussy juice is fresh?"

"Robert!" Bobbi squealed. She slapped him on the arm and flounced onto her other side so that her back was toward him.

Bob just laughed and took another drink. He and Longarm shared the pail until it was empty, then Bob set it aside, retrieved his lamp, and said, "You two have fun now, y'hear?" He left, pulling the door closed behind him.

"Sometimes . . . I swear," Bobbi grumbled, affection for her brother clear in her tone of voice.

Longarm chuckled. Then became serious as Bobbi got things going again by wriggling low on the bed so she could take Longarm's limp and sticky pecker into her mouth.

It did not take long for him to catch up with her.

Chapter 46

"Pass that pail, somebody."

"Anyone for another?"

"Another what?"

"You have a dirty mind."

"Yes, I do. What's your excuse?"

The three of them—Bob Temple, Jake Scott, and the fellow they knew as Nathan James—laughed uproariously, far out of proportion to the comments of the moment. But then they had been drinking for two days straight, only taking a few hours at night to fall asleep or minutes during the day to eat the meals Bobbi prepared for them.

"Woman, go get us some more beer," Bob ordered.

"I don't have any money, damn you. You've already drunk up my entire household budget for the month."

"Here," Longarm said. He fished around in his pants pockets, found a pair of double eagles, and handed them to Bobbi. "Use these."

"That is way too much," she protested. But he noticed she did take the coins and drop them into her apron pocket.

"Use the chance for some food. You know. T' fill out that household budget you was mentioning."

Once Bobbi was on her way, Jake leaned back and said,

"Damn, I am gonna miss you boys. In my business, well, I ain't had much chance to make real friends."

"I feel the same, partner," Bob said with a sigh and a shake of his head.

"Where are you going that you're gonna miss us?" Longarm asked. He reached into his pocket, pulled out a slightly bent but still intact cheroot, and lighted it.

"North," Jake said. "I promised a man I'd haul another load of Chinks."

"Chinks? What the hell do they have to do with it?" Bob asked, reaching for their last pail that still held any beer.

"You know. Chinese. I do some work for a fella that smuggles them across the border. There's some Mexicans that bring them up this far, then another fella that collects them from the Mexes, then if they get clear of the border without any trouble, I take over and drive them up north to the fella who set all this up."

"What does he do with them?" Longarm asked, genuinely curious.

"He has him a coal mine. He works some of the Chinks his own self and sells the rest of them to whatever mines want to buy them. I guess they're good workers. Don't have to be paid shit and if they die"—Jake shrugged—"they die. No harm done. They're perfect for those unstable mines up there."

"I wish you wouldn't go. You could join Nathan and me when we hit that bank down in Mexico," Bob said. "It's ripe to be took. Payday for the Mexes is coming up in a few days. I know. I keep track of this shit."

Longarm took a drag on his cheroot and a pull at the beer pail and mused, "You know, boys, I got some business to take care of up in Colorado. It occurs to me that maybe you, Jake, an' you, Bob, could go partners on the bank, an' I could deliver your Chinks for you, Jake."

"That wouldn't be fair, Nathan. The bank will bring in a helluva lot more than hauling a few lousy Chinese would."

"Like I said, I got business up there anyway. This would get the Chinese delivered to where they're s'posed to be an' still leave you boys free t' put all that payroll money in your pockets."

"We could cut you in for a share, Nathan. That would be the fair thing to do," Bob said.

"You're a good man, Temple." Longarm meant that. He liked Bob and would have hated to arrest him. This idea would get him well away from the border so that he did not have to know what they did. Or when. "But I wouldn't take a full share for not doing a full share o' the work. Nor taking a full share o' the risk."

"Ten percent then?"

Longarm nodded. "Aye, I think that'd be fair."

Jake leaned forward. He looked excited. "I'm suppose to meet the next group day after tomorrow. If you're serious about this, Nathan . . ."

"I'm serious, Jake."

Jake slapped his knee. "Splendid. That settles it. Nathan can take my Chinese and I'll help Bob take his bank."

"Woman! Where's that beer?"

"I'm coming, damnit," Bobbi responded from the back door where she was just coming in, heavily laden with fresh pails of pilsner.

Longarm noticed the way Jake sat up a little straighter and looked more attentive when Bobbi Temple was near. He suspected that once he was on his way north with those Chinese, wherever it was they were headed, it would not be too terribly long before Jake took his place in Bobbi's bed.

That was just fine. Longarm was not in love with the girl, but he suspected Jake was.

He supposed he should try to stop the two from robbing that bank, and if it were an American bank, he would. But the laws down in Mexico had nothing to do with his duties as a deputy U.S. marshal. The way he figured it, the Mexicans could look out for themselves. He had business to finish up here.

"Let me have one o' them pails, Bobbi honey," he said, grinning and reaching for the beer.

Chapter 47

"You can handle a six-up, can't you?" Jake asked Longarm as they were preparing to go collect the Chinese.

Longarm nodded. "Sure can." And, hell, who knew. Maybe he could. He could manage a team of four horses. How much worse could six be? He did not mention to the stocky teamster that he had never actually *tried* to drive a team of six.

"All right then. Here we go." Jake paused outside a barn about three miles north of El Paso. He whispered, "This is where we pick 'em up from the bull crews and transfer them to horse-drawn outfits. Faster that way, of course."

"Of course," Longarm agreed.

Jake glanced around to make sure there was no one else in sight, then tapped four times on the door, opened it and slipped inside. Longarm followed close behind him.

The man inside was slender, with a straggly blond mustache that looked like a cat could lick it off. He also carried a sawed-off 12-gauge double barrel. He held it leveled at the door until he saw who was there. Then he dropped the muzzles only a little.

"Who's this, Jake?"

"He's my new swamper. I hurt my back the other day.

Nathan will help me with the team. Don't worry about him though. He's a friend. You can trust him."

"If you say so, but what will Mr. Dolan say?"

"Leave that to me," Jake assured the man with the shotgun. Then he stepped to the side and half turned. He said, "Nathan, this here is Johnny Oakes. Johnny, this 's Nathan James."

"James? Say are you . . . ?"

"No relation," Longarm said quickly. Damn but he had been stupid to pick James for his last name.

"All right then. Shake." Oakes stepped forward and offered his hand. Much preferable to the shotgun, Longarm figured. He shook the thin man's hand.

"Where's your Chinks?" Jake asked.

"Over here. I got 'em bundled into the last two stalls there."

Longarm could not see any Chinese but he could see the heads of six large horses peeking over the walls of the other stalls.

"The wagon is parked out back," Jake explained, "along with Johnny's wagon and bull team."

Longarm nodded.

"Is there anything else you need from me?" Oakes asked.

"No, sir, we can take it from here, I think. Can we help you hook up?"

Oakes shook his head. "I'm all ready to roll. Hitched them just after dawn today."

"The Chinks giving you any trouble?"

"Naw, not now. Last night, middle of the night some time, one of them started giving me some shit and wouldn't calm down. The others were getting rattled, too, so I shot the troublemaker and dumped him in the road. That shut them up, let me tell you. Haven't have a lick of trouble out of them since."

"Hopefully the message will take and there won't be any more trouble out of them."

"I'm gonna take off now. It will take me half the day to get these slow movers home." Oakes shook hands again all around. Longarm and Jake trailed him out back of the barn to where he had his bull team already hitched to a large, empty wagon.

They saw Oakes off, then Jake said, "Come on, Nathan. Let me introduce you to these boys of mine. Pay close attention, mind you. Each of them has his own spot in the hitch and they won't go well for you if you get them mixed up."

"Of course. You, uh, you are gonna tell me where I'm s'posed to be takin' these Chinks, aren't you?"

Jake grinned and patted his shirt pocket. "I got it all written down for you. Where you go. Who you see there. All that shit."

Longarm chuckled and bobbed his head. "Then let's get started, friend. I got a long way t' go with these heathens."

"Mind how Johnny took care of things, Nathan," Jake said while he picked up a set of harness and draped it over his shoulder. "If any of them gives you any shit, just shoot him. In the head is best. That puts them down cold. Say, have you ever shot anybody before?"

Longarm shook his head. "No, I ain't."

"Well, what you got to keep in mind is that these is Celestials. They ain't like human beings. They're just Chinks, and Chinks don't count as people."

"I'll try and remember that, Jake," Longarm solemnly assured the man.

"Now grab ahold of that set of harness there and I'll introduce you to my boys."

Longarm did what he was told. Even with the two of them working—and Longarm fumbling his way through the process—it took the better part of an hour to get all six horses in harness and hitched in their proper places.

Jake dropped the ponderous tailgate on the big freight wagon and said, "All right, Nathan. Time to herd those

Celestials into the wagon. And remember, It should take you about four days, maybe five to get to Ludlow. You say you know where that is?"

"For the twelfth time, Jake, yes, I know where Ludlow is."

"All right then. Don't let any of the Chinks out of the wagon until you deliver them to Mr. Dolan. Tell him I'm sick or something. He'll pay you, then you can bring the team and wagon back." Jake smiled. "By then me and Bob should be rich men. And you'll have a share. You have our word on that."

"Fair enough, Jake."

The stocky smuggler motioned for Longarm to follow, then opened the first of the two stalls where the Chinese were being confined. "Out. Everybody out." He crooked a finger, and there was a clatter of chains.

Longarm blinked. He had not expected this.

The Chinese who filed awkwardly out of the stall were shackled, each with a pair of ankle rings joined by a seven or eight foot section of light chain that they carried.

"Into the wagon now. Everybody in." Jake mimed the action he wanted and the dozen Chinese climbed into the wagon bed. He positioned them along one side of the wagon, took up a heavier chain that was attached to the forward wall of the wagon bed, and wove that through the men's legs so that they were all essentially chained together even though they had some limited freedom of movement by way of the lighter chain on their feet.

"Now you bring out the rest of them," Jake said to Longarm. "Do just like I done."

Longarm did. Reluctantly. Chains were for dogs, he figured, not for people. The truth was that he wanted this Dolan person more than ever now.

Once all twenty-four Chinese were linked, Jake used a heavy padlock to join the two heavy chains. He closed the lock and handed the key to Longarm. "Don't lose this," he cautioned. "I did once and caught hell for it."

They fastened the tailgate shut and Longarm asked, "What about food and breaks so they can shit?"

"Sons of bitches are in there; they can stay until you get to Ludlow. They'll be fine. Trust me."

"If you say so."

"Aye, I do."

Longarm offered his hand to the stocky man. "Good luck down south."

"And you, up north there."

Longarm climbed onto the driver's seat of the ten-foot-tall wagon and very nervously picked up the driving lines. A six-up! How the hell did he get into this situation anyhow.

"Hiyup," he called, shaking what he hoped were the leaders' lines. The six big horses started forward.

"Take care, Nathan. Take care." Longarm did not look back to acknowledge Jake's farewell; he was too busy, and too worried, handling those six unfamiliar cobs.

Chapter 48

Longarm worried about the Chinese he was transporting north into the United States where they most assuredly did not belong. According to the laws of the U.S. they were criminals. More or less. There were some gray areas there the way things were now written. What was not in question was that they were human beings.

Not a one of them could speak a word of English, he discovered, but they were appreciative when he daily handed out food purchased along the way and water that he stored in gourds that he gave to them.

The men—they were all male, he found, destined for the coal mines of southern Colorado—were frighteningly silent. As far as he could tell not a one of them spoke except to obsequiously bow and yammer whenever he did anything for them.

Longarm stopped in Canutillo long enough to send a telegraph to Marshal Billy Vail in Denver. He told the boss what he intended and asked for backup in Ludlow when he got there as well as asking Henry to look into someone there named Dolan. Since he was away from their planned El Paso deception he signed the wire with his real name, dropping the ill-chosen alias Nathan James.

REPLY BERINO WITH INSTRUCTIONS, he concluded the message.

"That'll be seventy-five cents," the telegrapher told him after reading over the message form.

Longarm could have had the wire charged to the government but that would have meant digging out his badge, still buried inside the leather of his holster, and he did not want to take time for that. He paid the bill out of pocket instead and reminded himself to put it on his expense voucher.

Berino was half a day's run north of Canutillo. He reached it past noon, paused to distribute water and tortillas to the Chinese, then headed to the village's telegraph office, located in a corner of a combination cantina and mercado.

The telegrapher at least spoke passable English, a find that was something of an accomplishment around here.

"You have a message for Custis Long?"

"*Sí.*"

"I'd like it, please."

"You have identification?"

"No. But I have a dollar. Will that do?"

"Three dollars will."

Longarm grumbled but he felt he had no choice. He was completely out of the money Henry had advanced him and had not thought to replenish his cash supply back in El Paso where he could have drawn against the Nathan James account set up for him there. Now it was too late for that and he was getting into his own funds, both for the telegrams and to take care of the Chinese who were in his charge.

He forked over a five-dollar gold piece, took two silver pesos in change, and accepted the folded message form.

He scowled and kicked a nearby keg of nails when he read it.

CUSTIS LONG IS DEAD STOP WHO ARE YOU QUERY

Damnit, hadn't Danny or one of those other rangers thought to tell Billy Vail that his top deputy was in fact *not* dead like the newspapers claimed?

For that matter, why the hell hadn't he thought to send such a wire? He could have done that. From a different telegraph office rather than the one where they knew him as N. James, of course, but he could have told Billy he was still alive and not rotting in some distant eddy on the Rio Grande.

He just had not thought to do it.

Apparently it was a little too late now.

Longarm bought himself some jerky, an apple, and a plump cigar then went out and climbed back onto the driving box of the big wagon that was hauling his illegals. He had miles to cover . . . and no help waiting when he got there.

Chapter 49

Two days later Longarm and his coffle of Chinese reached the town of Las Vegas. The lack of a welcoming response from Billy Vail had been gnawing at him ever since they pulled out of Berino. He decided that he just damned well *had* to contact Billy again.

He stopped at a stock tank just south of town. There was a windmill drawing from the sands of what he guessed would be the now-dry bed of the upper Conchas River. Obviously there was still some water beneath the surface, enough to feed the windmill pump.

The mill was turned off at the moment so Longarm climbed the tower and tugged the pull to engage the fan and begin to pump water. Within a few minutes the first cold, refreshing water poured out into the stagnant algae-scummed water that lay an inch or two deep in the bottom of the clay tank.

Longarm felt hot, gritty, and dried out after the slow, sunbaked trip up from El Paso. He crawled down off the wagon, stripped and bathed himself under the now-icy flow. He felt infinitely better once he was bathed and had his clothes back on even if those articles of clothing were limp and smelly from too much use.

He thought about it for a moment, then brought out his key and unlocked the Chinese. He left one long chain free but locked the other side again. It might not be a very good idea to allow half of his charges to be loose behind his back.

The first stick he motioned to the ground. It was the first the men had had a chance to set foot on solid earth in three days.

Using hand signals and a bit of pantomime he had the men, still wearing their ankle chains, walk into the tank and wash away some of the filth under the cold running water.

They smiled and jabbered in what he assumed was appreciation—for all he knew they could have been cussing him and all his ancestors—once they were done.

He put that lot back into the wagon, chained them again, and let the other half come out and do the same thing. Again he received smiles in response even though they could have used their chains as weapon and ganged up on him if they wanted to.

And these were men who were being carried into slavery.

Not that they knew it. And not that he was going to do it.

"All right, everybody back into the wagon." The Chinese could not understand his words, but his gestures moved them along. They willingly climbed back into the bed of the big wagon and chained themselves up again.

Longarm affixed the lock on the chains and lifted the heavy tailgate back in place, shutting the Chinese into what by now was a thoroughly stinking box.

He did notice that they somehow managed to ride hidden there for three days without accumulating any shit on the floor. They must have been collecting it and tossing it out as they went. He hoped they did not throw any turds at any of the good citizens of the towns they passed through.

Once in Las Vegas he turned away from the main road and drove to the central plaza. He kept his smelly wagon full of illegal immigrants across the square from the elegant

Plaza Hotel, parked, and walked to the Western Union office that was attached to the grand hotel. Mighty convenient
for registered guests, he supposed.

"Yes, sir?"

"I want t' send a telegram."

The clerk slid a message form across the counter.

"I expect I'll be needin' more than that little bitty sheet
t' say all I want to," Longarm told the man. He got a handful of the small, yellow sheets back and a pen with a copper
nib and bottle of prepared ink. "Let me know when you're
ready."

Longarm glanced at the ink bottle and grinned, then he
nodded and bent over the message forms.

henry comma remember the time you spilled ink on
billy's stetson query who was it that snuck it out of the office and replaced the damn thing before he ever found out
query and who was it that covered your bet last month
when you foolishly drew to an inside straight and caught
the eight you needed query and who is it that always repays
any loans you make query now will you for god's sake tell
billy that it really is me down here needing help when I
deliver these chinese in ludlow stop mark's name may I say
again may be named dolan or that may be an alias stop just
in case something happens and billy's best deputy don't
make it home stop now tell him goddamnit stop

"I think that should do it," Longarm said, handing over
the two forms he had used.

The clerk read the message and frowned. "We don't
transmit cussing," he declared. "This will have to come out.
And this. I'm not so sure about this," he said, pointing to
the word "snuck."

"What the hell's the matter with snuck?"

"I don't think it is correct grammar. I can look it up if
you like."

"No, damnit, I don't like. Just leave it be. But come to
think of it I need t' add something." He pulled a third form

over, dipped the nib of the pen into the ink again and wrote:
RETURN C/O CUSTIS LONG WESTERN UNION RATON NM STOP

The clerk counted up the words and clucked his tongue. "That is an awfully expensive wire. Would you like me to shorten it for you?"

"No, damnit, I just want you t' send it. Just exactly the way it is."

"I'm afraid that will be . . ."

"That will be," Longarm interrupted, "collect. Send it out collect to United States Marshal William Vail, Federal Building, Colfax Avenue, Denver, Colorado."

"Collect?"

Longarm nodded. Firmly. "Collect."

"Yes, sir. Collect."

Longarm shoved a quarter across the counter as a tip, then turned and went out to collect his Chinese once again.

Chapter 50

"Nathan. Nathan James."

He stopped and let go of the hitching line he'd just picked up. Now who the hell in Las Vegas would know him? He turned. And took his hat off. "Amanda. How very nice to see you again." He smiled and bobbed his head. "You're looking well."

That was damn sure the truth. The girl looked prettier than ever. Younger, too, he thought.

He saw her and immediately remembered her naked. Lordy, but she was one fine little piece of tail. The night they had spent together up in Trinidad . . . his pecker remembered even better than he did. It leaped to attention and began pushing at the buttons of his fly, wanting out so it could go play with Amanda.

She saw and laughed but mercifully refrained from pointing. After all, there were people on the plaza who might see.

"It's nice to see you, too, Nathan."

"I, uh . . ." He was not sure what to say to the girl. Hell, he hadn't ever expected to see her again. For sure he was not going to apologize for taking her cherry. That had been more than pleasant. And her idea anyway.

"I've missed you, Nathan."

She stepped down off the boards of the sidewalk and walked into the street to take his arm and hold it tight beneath hers. "Aren't you going to kiss me hello?"

"Right here? In public?"

"Oh, a peck on the cheek between old friends should be all right."

"Of course." He bent down and gave her the requested peck. "It's really good to see you, Amanda." It occurred to him that he should be glad his Chinese had a chance to bathe before they rolled into town lest the smell of them gag Amanda and drive her away. Not that the wagon smelled any too damn good as it was, but it was a sight better than it had been.

Inside the wagon bed there was some thumping and rattling of movement.

"What are you hauling there, Nathan?"

"Oh, uh, a load o' hogs, that's all."

"Smelly things, aren't they," Amanda sniffed.

"Sure. I, uh . . ."

"I'm glad I ran into you today, Nathan. I have a problem you could help me with." She looked at him through lowered eyelids. Very prettily, he thought, and shy. Which had to be so much bullshit; Amanda was not shy, as he remembered very well. "Will you help me, Nathan?"

"I, uh . . ."

"It is important. Not the sort of thing I could discuss with my sister though. I would be much too embarrassed."

"I suppose. Sure." The Chinese had just been cleaned up and watered and fed. They should be all right where they were for long enough that he could see what Amanda wanted and maybe help her with it if it was not too complicated a problem she was having.

"Walk with me, Nathan." Amanda led the way across the plaza and down one of the side streets for two blocks before she turned into an alley. She stopped in front of a small barn and said, "In here."

Longarm grunted, thinking more of his Chinese sitting there baking in the hot midday sun than he was about Amanda and her problems. He took hold of the big door and slid it aside two or three feet. "All right?"

"Yes, thank you. Come inside, please."

He followed her into the cool, shadowy interior of the little carriage house. He was surprised when Amanda reached behind him and tugged the door closed. Then she was in his arms, her lips locked on his and her tongue halfway down his throat.

"Nathan honey, I haven't been laid even once since I got here. All I've been able to think of was that prick of yours and how good it felt inside me. Fuck me again, Nathan. Please. Take me again."

"Amanda, I . . ." How the hell do you tell a girl that you don't have time to lift her skirts because you have a bunch of . . . what had he told her . . . a bunch of hogs waiting in a wagon on the plaza.

Not that he had time to tell her anything, actually. Before Longarm could think of what excuse he might make, Amanda was on her knees in the straw, her fingers busily—and quite expertly—working on his fly.

She had his cock out and into her mouth in a matter of seconds.

It was not the sort of thing a man could very well object to.

And, oh, it did feel good.

The wet heat of her enveloped him as she tried to swallow him, taking his length nearly balls deep into her throat.

Longarm staggered half a pace back and braced himself against the door while Amanda sucked and pulled at his cock and fondled his balls none too gently in both hands.

Finally she came up for air, grinned up at him, and winked. "My goodness but I've missed this since you left. Did you miss me, too?"

"I sure did, honey," he lied. The truth was that he had not

thought of her once since the last time he saw her. "I missed you somethin' awful."

"Come here, Nathan." The girl jumped to her feet, rose onto tiptoes to plant a quick kiss on him and took him by the hand. "Over here."

There was a pile of fresh straw against the wall to their left. Amanda led him there and presented herself for another kiss, then lifted her skirts and spread herself on the straw for him. She was not wearing any underthings. Her pussy winked pink and dripping wet.

He really had no time, but . . .

Longarm dropped down and wedged in between her legs while he pushed his britches down to his knees.

Amanda sighed with happiness when Longarm's hard prick speared and filled her. "That's what I've been missing, Nathan." She giggled. "I think I love you. At least a little." She giggled again.

Longarm paid no attention to her giggling. He concentrated instead on the feel of sliding inside that sweet pussy and out again. Little Amanda was still awfully tight, and his Chinese could just wait a bit. Long enough for this . . . and maybe for one more time.

The rush of sensation began to build deep inside his balls and Longarm increased his speed, pumping harder, deeper, faster.

Amanda cried out and clutched him tight as she wrapped her legs around his waist.

With a grunt of effort he poured his cum into her.

"God, am I ever glad I ran into you today, Nathan. No, don't pull out yet. I like to feel it there. Leave it where it is for a minute or two."

In another minute or two he would be hard and ready to go again, he knew.

He doubted little Amanda would mind.

Chapter 51

"Now looka here, darlin', it's getting late in the day. I could stay here overnight an' drive on north tomorrow." He leaned down and gave her nipple a flick of his tongue in case she mistook his meaning and needed a sort of reminder.

"You know I would love to do exactly that, Nathan, but the family would be in an uproar if I stayed out all night. My sis would tell Daddy and then there would be hell to pay. Why, if he ever found out about you, he'd surely hire someone to come shoot you. No, I'm afraid you'll have to spend tonight with just those handsome horses for company." She sighed, then patted his cheek. "But I will for sure be thinking of you, Nathan. And of this." Amanda reached down and squeezed his now-limp cock and his balls, all in one affectionate gesture. Which was nice but not exactly what Longarm had had in mind for later.

In truth it was only about the middle of the afternoon or a little later. He could still put some miles behind them.

"You are a darling girl, Amanda . . . uh . . . damnit, this is embarrassing but I've forgot your last name."

Rather than take offense Amanda found that admission to be hilarious. She laughed heartily and did not answer him until she was able to get control of herself again. "Crocker, dear. My name is Amanda Sue Crocker."

"I won't forget it again," Longarm said. "I can promise you that."

"I should hope so," Amanda sniffed. "I would be terribly disappointed if you ever forget me."

"Never. I swear it. Now turn loose o' me so's I can make myself presentable." He laughed. "Even after all we been doing this afternoon all you gotta do is stand up an' pull your dress down."

"This seems to be the one occasion when a mere woman has the advantage over a man." Amanda stood, pushed her skirts down and brushed the straw stems off her clothing. "There," she said. "I'm all ready. You go on and get yourself dressed, Nathan. I'll go ahead back to my sister's house, but thank you for the fuck. It was fun. Bye-bye."

With a quick wave of her hand and a swirl of her skirts, Amanda Sue Crocker was out the door and gone.

Longarm shook his head with amusement. That little girl was a caution.

But she sure as hell took to this screwing like a real pro.

He knelt and rooted through the straw for his gun belt. It seemed to have somehow been buried during their exertions.

He got himself buttoned, tucked, and properly belted, then brushed his brand-new Stetson off—damn thing looked all right but it still didn't feel quite as comfortable as the one he had lost in the Rio Grande—and sidled out the carriage house door.

A gaggle of little boys playing marbles in the alley seemed a mite startled to see him appear there, but they said nothing and Longarm was quickly back out onto the street.

He got his bearings and strode back to the big wagon that was standing ready by the plaza. He collected the hitch weights, climbed onto the driving box, and took up the lines, ignoring the Chinese who were huddled silent and still in the back of the wagon.

There were still several hours of daylight remaining, and he might as well make the best of them.

Chapter 52

Raton, New Mexico, was small but bustling with noise and activity as freight outfits moved both ways through the pass. Those would disappear once the railroad reached this far south, but for now they carried the lifeblood of commerce in their wagons and on the backs of their mules.

Longarm and his freight wagon were just one more in the crowd.

"Who you hauling for?" one friendly teamster called up to Longarm, perched high above the street on the seat of the big wagon.

"Fella name of Bomer down in Albuquerque," Longarm lied.

"I don't know him."

"Good fella. Good man to work for," Longarm embellished the first lie.

"Think he'd hire me?" the man persisted.

"I dunno. He might. If you look him up, tell him Don Childs sent you." Longarm had heard of a D. Childs once. He saw the name on a wanted poster a long time ago.

"That's mighty kind of you, Mr. Childs. Thanks. I, uh, don't suppose you could use a helper for the rest of your run. I'm good at greasing axles and working horses and whatever

needs to be done. I got a strong back for loading or unloading. If you need somebody, that is."

"Not this trip but . . . what's your name, mister?"

"Sohn." He spelled it out so Longarm might remember.
"Edgar Sohn, Mr. Childs."

"Pleasure t' meet you, Edgar. Now if you'll excuse me,
I got t' get under way. It's a long, hard pull to the top and I
wanta have some horses left in front of me when I get there."

"I understand that, Mr. Childs. Good luck to you."

"And t' you, Mr. Sohn." Longarm touched a forefinger to
the brim of his Stetson, shook out his lines, and drove on
toward the edge of town and the start of the rugged climb toward the top of Raton Pass.

Miles of agonizing switchbacks later—agonizing to the
horses anyway and no ball of fun to Longarm, either—they
crested the top of the pass. Ahead of them, some thousands
of feet below, lay Trinidad and the rolling hills of Colorado
while to the west was a wall of rugged mountains.

It was too late in the day and the road too treacherous to
attempt a descent. They would have to wait until daybreak
for that. Longarm hated to keep his Chinese penned up
where they were but he had no choice about it. There were
too many other wagons, mule trains and travelers around to
see should he bring them out. They would just have to stay
where they were.

A Concord stagecoach came bumping and swaying up
from the Colorado side and went past in a rush. Longarm
smiled, thinking of the trip down taken with Amanda
Crocker at his side. Their night in Trinidad had been . . .
memorable.

And the afternoon in Las Vegas hadn't been too damn
bad, either.

He began to get a hard-on just thinking about the girl.
This was neither the time nor the place for that sort of
thing, so he forced himself to think about the big horses in
his hitch.

He was becoming used to the sturdy animals and was even reasonably comfortable with the wealth of lines he had to handle to drive a six-up. Driving two was nothing; driving four was easy, but six was an experience almost as memorable as screwing young Miss Crocker had been. If in a slightly different way, of course.

Longarm pulled his rig off the road as far away from others as he could manage, then climbed down and tied the horses around the sides of the wagon. He saw to their feeding, then built himself a fire. He boiled a can of coffee and laced it thick with condensed milk and brown sugar before soaking some slabs of hardtack in the tan-colored mixture. He had had worse meals and in fact found this one to be rather good.

After a supper he did not dare share with his Chinese, he had a cup of black coffee to wash things down and then polished the meal off with a cigar.

Belly full and arm weary after handling six pairs of heavy leathers all day, he kicked the fire apart and climbed back onto the driving box of the wagon. He lay down on the mud-crusted floor of the driving box and settled in for the night.

Chapter 53

Longarm got an early start in the morning. And why not. There was certainly no comfort to be found in lying abed any later.

He made a cold breakfast of leftovers from last night's dinner, then carefully—he had to get the horses' order in the hitch just right or he would have an equine mutiny on his hands—rebuilt the hitch for the final pull down onto the plains.

The Chinese were still sleeping when he put the six-up in motion but the bumping and jarring soon had them awake and whispering among themselves. It occurred to him to wonder what they thought they were being taken toward. Not slavery, he was fairly certain of that.

When the grade steepened he pulled to a halt, climbed down, and chained each back wheel so it could not roll. That way the wagon could not roll up on the hocks of the wheelers, which was a sure way to wind up with broken legs. Once the chains were in place the team would have to pull, even going downhill.

He kept the chains in place until he neared the bottom of the pass where "Uncle Dick" Wootton's now-abandoned tollhouse stood. The old mountain man had made a good

living from his toll road for many years before he finally
sold out to the railroad. Longarm had heard that the old
man was retired now and living in Trinidad with his third
wife. Or maybe she was his fifth, Longarm really was not
sure. He only hoped the old man was happy in his retire-
ment. Wootton was certainly entitled to that after a long and
often dangerous career. Few of his peers had survived so
long. Or so well.

The railroad had progressed two miles or more since
Longarm went south. Before long it would be possible to
ride the rails from Denver all the way to El Paso.

Modern marvels! Longarm shook his head in wonder at
the thought.

He drove past Trinidad and on the few miles north to the
siding at Ludlow. He parked in front of the rickety little
general store that, along with a very few other buildings sat
just outside the boundaries of the Colorado Fuel and Iron
property. On the other side of that invisible line were coal
mines, company housing, and a company store where
workers or their families could buy supplies at outrageous
prices . . . but without needing actual cash. They bought on
credit against future earnings. The smart workers were the
ones who came outside company property and bought from
Hart Torrington, who ran the independent store.

Longarm left his Chinese where they were and climbed
the steps to the platform that ran across the storefront. There
were two old men sitting in rocking chairs. One of them,
damnit, was Uncle Dick. Longarm had met the man in line
of work several years earlier. He hoped to hell Wootton either did not remember him or had eyesight too faded with
age to keep him from recognizing Longarm as a deputy
United States marshal.

To head off Wootton, just in case, Longarm announced,
"My name's Nathan James. I'm here lookin' for a man name
of Dolan. I got a delivery for him."

The man who had been jawing with Wootton stood and

gave Longarm a suspicious looking over. "Where's the regular man?" he demanded.

"Jake had other business he had t' take care of. He sent me instead."

"Your name is James, you say?"

"Yes, and before you ask, no, I'm no relation to them Jameses."

The fellow grunted and said, "You can pull your rig over to the north edge of the field there," he said, pointing to a broad stretch of grass that lay between the railroad tracks and a thirty- or forty-foot-tall wall of pale rock. "Stop inside that line of trees and wait. Somebody will come for you."

"All right," Longarm said.

The man—Longarm took him to be the proprietor, Torrington—went inside the store.

Dick Wootton crooked a finger and Longarm leaned down close to hear what the old man had to say.

In a hoarse whisper Wootton said, "Don't think I don't remember you. You're that deputy Long that was down in Trinidad a while back. Now you say your name is James so you must be working. That's fine. I won't say nothing against you."

"Thank you, sir." Longarm patted Wootton's forearm and gave the old mountain man a wink.

Torrington came back outside and said, "Somebody will meet you in about an hour. It's safe to unload those Chinks. Let them stretch their legs a little but keep them in chains. Don't want to take any chances with them this close to delivery, do you."

"Thanks. Is there water over there that I can give 'em?"

"There's a little brook comes down out of the rocks if you go over close to that wall of limestone."

"All right. You can tell your man that I'll park over there."

"Keep those Chinks chained, mind. We had a bunch of them scatter like quail one time a year or so ago. Never did get some of them back and the others were too spooked to be worth a shit in the mines."

"I'll take care," Longarm promised. He gave Wootton a small wave and went back to the wagon and his six-up. He was rather proud of being able to handle those big boys now. But it would not hurt his feelings any to get this smuggling business wrapped up so he could go back to Denver and be Custis Long again instead of a shady asshole named Nathan James.

"Hyup," he barked, shaking out the driving lines and pulling the horses around in a wide turn to head them back north again.

Chapter 54

He pulled the team close to the buff-colored wall of limestone, found the thin rill of water that flowed down from the
rock, formed a pool, and then disappeared into the ground
fifteen feet or so on.

Longarm left the horses to stand in harness while he let
down the tailgate of the big wagon and unlocked the Chinese. He motioned them out of the wagon.

The men came out chattering and broke into wide smiles
when they saw the water. Longarm motioned them toward
it to give them permission to bathe. Within seconds they
were naked except for their shackles and chains. To a man
they took turns sinking neck deep in the pool to cool and
cleanse themselves.

Longarm hadn't thought to buy food at Torrington's
store. All he had remaining in the wagon was a handful of
jerky, far from enough to go around to all the Chinese, and
he would not have felt comfortable eating now when they
had to go hungry. He settled for collecting a can full of icy
cold water from the spill above the pool. He drank a little,
then put the rest over a small fire to boil coffee.

He had finished drinking that can and was considering

boiling another when he saw a pair of horsemen come out of the CF&I property along the road that was—in theory at least—a public right of way. One of the two dropped off at the blacksmith shop beside Torrington's. The other came on toward Longarm and the wagon.

Time to go to work, Longarm figured. He stood, kicked his fire apart, and waited for the horsebacker to reach him.

"Mr. Sohn," Longarm said when the man stopped beside the wagon. "Edgar, right?"

"You have a good memory, Mr. Childs." He laughed. "Or is it Mr. James?"

"James, actually. So tell me. D'you know where I can find this Dolan fellow?"

The laughter increased. "I'm Dolan."

"Well, I'll be a son of a bitch."

"Aye, there's a lot of us around. Say, I want to tell you. The boss really liked the way you handled me back there at Raton. You never skipped a beat with those phony names and you never gave nothing away. You did just fine."

"Thanks, but . . . the boss, you say? I thought you was the boss, Dolan."

"Not exactly, but you're gonna meet him in just a little while. Now load your Chinks up . . . mind you chain them proper . . . and follow me. We have to go through the CF&I property and on to the other side. That's where our diggings are."

"Sure thing." Longarm gave a shout and motioned for the Chinese to get back into the wagon, which they obediently did. He padlocked the central chains in place, put the tailgate back up, and climbed back onto the driving box.

The six-up followed Dolan past Torrington's and around a sweeping curve to the right. There was an empty gatehouse—but no gate—just where the road started to climb into the foothills through a natural breech in the wall of limestone.

Beyond that were dozens of shanties, a company store, even a tiny, stone walled structure with a sign posted over the door saying JAIL. Apparently giant CF&I even took care of that for themselves.

Past the jail was a schoolhouse and beyond that the diggings. There was not much to be seen, all the work being done far underground, but there were mountains of coal waiting to be shipped. Black coal dust was everywhere. What once might have been a pretty little foothill valley was now starkly bare, all brown stone and black dust. Every last vestige of vegetation was gone, to the point that Longarm wondered if family gardens were not permitted on company property so as to force the workers and their families to trade at the company store and increase the company's profits. He would not put a scheme like that past them.

The six-up followed a jog in the road, dropped down to ford a small stream, and began to climb again.

Dolan reined back so he was riding beside Longarm. "The boss's mines are on the other side of this ridge here," he said, pointing to the rugged mass off to their right, to the north.

At least, Longarm noticed, there was a little vegetation now that they seemed to be off CF&I land, juniper and scrub oak and small cactus. It wasn't much, but at least it was green.

"How far to get there?" he asked Dolan.

The man grinned. "Another four miles or so before we can cross over and double back. You could do it on foot, of course, but there wouldn't be no way to get a wagon over. Nor even a horse, I wouldn't think."

Longarm glanced toward the sky, then said, "That should put us there before dark."

"Aye." Dolan waved for him to follow and spurred his horse into a trot.

Longarm clucked to his team and shook the lines, and

the big boys leaned into their harness and took a bone-jarring trot of their own.

Longarm looked around. Where the hell, he wondered, were Billy Vail and the boys. They should be here to back him up, shouldn't they?

Chapter 55

The mine the Chinese were headed toward was not much to look at. There was a commodious administration building, which Dolan said also housed the boss and his family. There was a spacious bunkhouse where the white overseers lived when they were on the site—they were allowed to take breaks in Trinidad now and then to get away from the pressures of work—and there was one very long, very low stone structure where the Chinese slaves, and they were indeed slaves, were housed under lock and key. Longarm had seen jails that were nicer and looked more comfortable. Hell, back in the day he had *been in* better jails himself.

They reached the mine just as dusk was spreading through the foothill canyons and gulleys.

"Stop here," Dolan told him. "I'll go tell the boss you're here and get some of the guards to take these Chinks off your hands."

"All right, thanks." Longarm sat perched on the tall driving box and took it all in. He was still wondering just where in hell Billy Vail and the boys might be. They were supposed to back him up, weren't they? So where the devil were they?

The man who emerged from the administration building was tall and thickset with muttonchop whiskers and a build that suggested he had been one powerful son of a bitch in his youth. Now he was gray and probably in his sixties. He was in shirtsleeves and hatless when he came out to greet Nathan James and the latest shipment of Chinese. He wore no pistol that Longarm could see but carried a rather wicked-looking riding crop that looked like it was half bat and the other half whip.

He approached the wagon and motioned for Longarm to climb down. Longarm set the brake on the rig and dropped to the ground. He walked forward and clipped a hitch weight to the bit of the off leader before he came back and offered his hand to the boss.

"Nathan James," he said. "Are you the man Jake told me to see up here?"

"I am. My name is Crocker, Mr. James. Aldous Egon Crocker. Mr. Dolan has told me good things about you. So has Mr. Scott." He gave Longarm a sly smile. "When Dolan told me there was a stranger driving the wagon I of course wired Scott to secure your bona fides. He tells me you are a good man, Mr. James. He also mentioned that he and someone . . . I forget that name . . . he and this other person have a tidy amount of cash that they owe you. He did not explain why."

"He couldn't," Longarm said. "Not over a telegraph wire that could be overheard by practically anybody."

"Yes, well, I assumed it was something like that. I'll not press you for details."

"Thank you." Obviously Jake and Bob Temple had succeeded in pulling off that robbery down in Mexico. Longarm supposed he should feel bad about that, but in truth he didn't. He liked Bob and Jake, and he figured it was up to the Mexicans to take care of the law down there. He had enough on his plate on this side of the border.

"May I ask you something, sir? A couple things, actually."

"You may ask. I may or may not tell you, depending."

"Fair enough. The first thing is, what d'you do with so

many Chinese? I understand there's a fairly steady flow of them. Surely you can't use them all in your own diggings here."

"Oh, I don't," Crocker said, flicking his quirt against his leg. "I have two other mines where I can use them myself, but having established this pipeline across the border it seemed a shame to let it go to waste bringing over only a few of the Celestials. I sell the surplus to others. Mines, short line railroads, wherever hard labor and frequent losses occur."

"Losses?" Longarm raised an eyebrow.

Again Crocker made that sly smile. "I think you know what I mean."

"Deaths," Longarm said.

Crocker shrugged. "Some loss is to be expected. At least with these devils there is no harm done when it happens."

"Of course," Longarm said. "I do have another question if you don't mind."

"Go ahead."

"It is about a certain young lady. Amanda Crocker. Would she happen to be . . ."

The mine owner tipped his head back and roared with laughter. "I wondered if you would be honest enough to mention that. Yes, Amanda is my daughter. And as a matter of fact, she mentioned you in a letter to her mother. She said a man named Nathan James met her on her way south and took her under his wing, so to speak. She said you acted as her protector on the trip."

"Yes, sir, that's true." Not the entire truth, of course. Not hardly.

"She said it was quite exciting speculating if you might be related to Frank and Jesse James."

"Sir, I told her that there's no relationship that I know of."

"Well, you know how young girls are."

"Yes, sir." Still no sign of Billy and the deputies, damnit. Surely he had enough on this man to put him behind bars for a tidy little stretch. He was sorry for Amanda that it had to happen, but that was the breaks. Surely Crocker knew the risk he was running when he got into this smuggling and slavery business. Now that he was caught, that was just the way it was.

While Longarm and Crocker had been talking a pair of guards had come out. They and Dolan stood quietly until they thought it a good time to interrupt the boss, then Dolan and one of the guards dropped the tailgate. The guard came over to Longarm.

"You got the key to that padlock?"

"Right here." Longarm produced the article and handed it to the man, but instead of immediately going to open the padlock he stood for a moment in the dying light, staring at Longarm.

"Is there something wrong?" Longarm asked.

The man shook his head, went and opened the lock, then returned and leaned close to Crocker to whisper something.

"Is that so, Tom? Thank you for telling me. Dolan, come here."

Tom went back to tending to the Chinese, unloading them and herding them into the stone barracks while Dolan hurried to his boss's side.

"Hand me your pistol," Crocker said.

"Yes, sir." Dolan handed it over without questioning the order.

Crocker immediately cocked the revolver and pointed it at Longarm's belly. "If there is anything I despise, it is a lawman, especially one who is not being honest in his duties. Get his pistol, Dolan. Then lock him up. Put him in the hole."

Chapter 56

The "pit" Crocker referred to was a hole perhaps six feet by six and six feet deep. It may originally been intended as a water sump or a cesspit but now served as a makeshift prison cell. An iron grate that may once have been a door lay over it, held in place by large stones, each of which would weigh several hundred pounds or more.

In order to open the pit Dolan had to call for help from several of the guards. Grunting with effort, the men rolled the stones back, then slid the grate aside to partially uncover the hole.

"In," Crocker ordered once the pit had been opened.

"Fuck you," Longarm said defiantly.

Crocker did not argue. He raised Dolan's revolver and took careful aim on Longarm's forehead. Dolan struck Longarm over the head with a fist-sized stone, perhaps saving his life. Longarm crumpled to the ground, where Dolan took hold of his legs and tumbled him into the pit. "All right, boys. Slide the cover back in place."

Longarm lay on the floor of the pit, one shoulder and arm lying in a shallow puddle of rainwater collected on one side of the floor.

He had no idea how long he lay there before he returned to consciousness, but it was some time after dark when he awakened. His arm ached from the cold water and his head was pounding from the blow Dolan had given him . . . but he was alive.

His hat and gun belt were missing although he did not remember anyone taking them nor giving them up before he was struck. The small amount of money he had was still in his pockets but his folding pocket knife was gone. His Ingersoll watch, with a custom-made derringer attached to the other end of the fob, was rather understandably missing, too.

Once he had taken stock of his own condition, he explored the pit as best he was able, the first priority being to determine first if there were any guards posted over him—there were not, the pit apparently being thought secure enough—and the second to determine if he could move the iron grate that trapped him in the hole.

Trying to move the grate proved to be about as easy as trying to pick up a small building. Try as he might, there was no way in hell he could lift, slide, or in any other way budge the damn thing.

He tried everything he could think of, to the point of near exhaustion, then sank down into a corner and tried to think this thing through.

Crocker was not keeping him here without purpose, he was sure. Either the man wanted something—information, although that seemed unlikely under the circumstances—or he did not want to murder a federal lawman in front of witnesses.

It would be one thing to abuse or even to kill a Chinese slave. It would be quite another to murder a deputy United States marshal.

There might be one or two guards, Dolan for instance, who Crocker would trust with that knowledge but widespread knowledge among all the guards, and the Chinese, too, since many of them would be moving on to other illicit slaveholders, would leave him open to gossip or blackmail.

Longarm had to assume that Crocker intended to kill him but somewhere else and outside the knowledge of all but a small handful of his employees.

He heard the crunch of gravel underfoot and looked up to see Crocker standing over the jail pit, his fine, patrician features highlighted by the pale light that came from a three-quarter moon.

"Something I can do for you?" Longarm drawled.

"Yes. As a matter of fact there is something I have been wanting to do to a lawman for quite some time," Crocker said.

"An' that would be . . . ?"

Crocker laughed. And began unbuttoning his fly.

Longarm had to step lively to avoid the stream of piss that splattered down through the grating above him.

Aldous Crocker laughed the whole way back to the administration building.

Longarm felt like committing murder himself. But only for a few moments. Then he realized that that son of a bitch Crocker was keeping him here for the pleasure of tormenting him. And that was good. It would give him time to figure a way out.

How much time though, Longarm asked himself. How much time did he have before Crocker tired of playing with him and decided to end his game?

He hunkered down in a corner of the pit, careful to avoid the rainwater on one side and the piss-dampened spots on another. He made no attempt to sleep though. He had to think. He had to prepare himself to act.

Just as soon as he figured out just what in hell that action was supposed to be.

Chapter 57

Dawn found Longarm close to exhaustion. More than that, however, much more, was the frustration that plagued him after spending the night pushing, pulling, and scratching at that son of a bitch iron grate. The thing was too heavy for him to move, no matter the desperation that fueled his strength, and it was too well constructed for him to dislodge any of the welded slats.

When it was barely light enough to see, Aldous Crocker came yawning and scratching himself to take another piss into the pit.

Longarm did not give the bastard the satisfaction of shouting the obscenities he was thinking.

Crocker laughed his way back inside.

Longarm saw no one for several hours after that. He heard shouting voices, some of them in Chinese, and the movement of a good many people, but none of them came near the prison pit. When the sounds of the Chinese died away into the distance Crocker appeared above him again along with a handful of guards. The grate was dragged aside and a short ladder was lowered into the pit.

"You can come out now."

Longarm considered balking at the instruction, but there

would have been no point in it. Down inside that hole he
could do nothing. Up on level ground he could hope for
some sort of opening that would lead to his escape.

Unfortunately both Crocker and Dolan were armed with
revolvers now while the other guards carried truncheons.
Crocker, Longarm saw, was carrying Longarm's own Colt.
Bastard! But he said nothing.

"Over there," Crocker said, pointing toward the long
building where the Chinese were housed.

"Fuck you," Longarm snarled.

"Look, James," Dolan responded, "you can do this easy or
you can do it hard. Your choice, but we're good at this. If you
walk over there like you're told, it won't go so hard on
you. If you sull up and get cranky, we'll beat you down to
your knees and carry you. But you do what you like."

James, he had said. So the hired help had not been told
who Longarm really was. Obviously one of them knew, that
one who told Crocker. But the rest were ignorant of the
facts. He had to wonder if they would act differently if they
found out.

Possibly, he conceded. But with no credentials he could
not prove a claim that he was a deputy U.S. marshal, and
Crocker was now wearing the holster where Longarm's
badge was hidden. Any appeal to them based on his being a
deputy would probably be ignored as a plea of desperation
rather than truth.

"Over there," Crocker said. "I won't tell you again."

Longarm did not like it, not by a damn sight, but he went
in the direction indicated.

When he got closer he saw why. Set high in the stone
wall were a number of steel rings, each with a set of manacles attached to them.

"Face the wall," Crocker ordered.

The men with the truncheons moved in closer, ready to
strike if he failed to comply.

He stepped to the wall and stood facing it.

"You know what to do."

When Longarm did not immediately lift his wrists to the manacles a hickory truncheon thudded hard over his right kidney. The pain was excruciating.

"Do it," the guard told him.

Longarm allowed himself to be chained to the stone wall.

Another guard stepped in and ripped his shirt away, exposing bare skin.

Crocker himself wielded the cat-o'-nine-tails, but the instrument was not nearly as painful as its appearance would indicate. A whip with one or only a few "tails" can cut to the bone. A cat with lead tips can do even worse. But this cat was constructed of ordinary leather tails. Feeling it was more like being pounded with a very heavy pillow than it was being actually whipped. Obviously the thing had never been used on any of these men, and the Chinese certainly would not have let on how ineffective a device it was. Longarm thought it only sensible that he keep the secret as well.

Even so it was damned annoying and after a while it hurt rather badly.

Crocker kept up the pounding until his arm got tired, then he let Dolan administer some blows. Finally they unchained Longarm and took him back to the pit.

They had not asked him a single question nor said anything about why they were doing this. Obviously Aldous Crocker was just having a good time at Custis Long's expense.

They dropped him back into the pit and again slid the iron grate over the opening.

Longarm was more determined than ever to get out of this damned pit, and when he did he intended to come nose to nose with that bastard Crocker.

Just as soon as he could figure out how he was going to do it.

Chapter 58

Longarm sat hunkered against the wall, feeling pretty much like shit. If this were a storybook, Amanda Sue would come home and—Pocahontas-like—rescue him from Daddy.

Unfortunately this was no storybook and the delectable Amanda was not due back until her sister had her kid, whenever that proved to be. Pity, he thought.

He leaned his head back against the wall. A thin rain of coarse grit fell out of his hair and onto his chest.

Now that he was thinking about it he realized there was grit caked in the sweat on his back and shoulders, too. He reached up and scrubbed a hand through his hair. Gray and black granules fell over his chest and into his lap.

He took the tatters that remained of his shirt and ran the cloth to and fro over his back. He could feel the granules there, too.

Now where in hell had all that come from, he wondered.

He scrubbed at his back some more and collected as much of the stuff as he could. There was no mystery about what it was. It was the exact same grit that had gotten into his hair.

But where . . . ?

Longarm peered up toward the top of the pit wall. He

could not see anything unusual there, but there was no question that the grit had to drop from *somewhere*.

He stood and looked closer. The grit that had fallen onto him seemed to be some of the same stuff the wall was made of.

He had thought—all right, assumed—that the wall was a dark sandstone. Instead it was a hard-packed clay base soil that contained the tiny spicules of stone or mica. They must have been dislodged onto Longarm's head when the grate was slid back in place.

Longarm grinned. And took inventory of everything he had on him.

After a few minutes he removed his belt and unthreaded the big, brass buckle from it.

Chapter 59

His hand had cramps so bad it was all he could do to keep from screaming, the result of holding that buckle and scratching away at the hard soil hour after hour.

He could see progress, though. That was the important thing. By gouging dirt away near the top of the wall he was able to create a small hole. Then a larger one, cutting it just beneath the iron grate.

The question was whether he could make his rabbit hole large enough for him to squeeze his shoulders through. Actually there was no question any longer whether he could do it. But could he do it before daybreak?

About four o'clock, judging by the stars, Longarm thought he just might have a wide enough hole.

Arms leading the way, shoulders following, belly sucked in and boots jammed against the iron slats of the grate, Custis Long slithered into the hole he had so laboriously dug.

His hands still hurt like hell, but he did not want to delay his escape attempt lest someone come wandering by—that bastard Crocker, for instance—and discover his labors prematurely. The best he could manage was to flex his fingers a few times, then make his way into the hole.

The first attempt failed. He could not twist upward at a

sharp-enough angle to permit him to pass through the tight restriction underneath the cold iron of the grate. He had to back out, retrieve the belt buckle, and dig some more.

Another half hour and his hand felt like it was permanently cramped. But the hole was bigger.

Big enough?

Longarm tried again to force himself through the narrow opening.

He was able to get his head above ground level outside of the pit. Some furious squirming got him the rest of the way into the chill predawn air, his shoulders ending up scraped and bloody, but the blood only served to lubricate his exit.

Longarm crawled slowly and painfully to his feet, a free man again.

Practically every square inch of skin was scraped. Practically every joint and muscle ached abominably.

But he was free, damnit. Free.

There were horses in a corral not far away, and the way to Denver was wide-open. Would be for another half hour or so until the Chinese were rousted out of their quarters.

Far and away the most sensible thing for Custis Long to do would be to head for Denver, collect Billy and the boys, and come larruping back down here as fast as they could move.

That would be sensible, Longarm acknowledged.

Instead he headed for the administration building where Aldous Crocker should still be sleeping.

Chapter 60

The front door was not locked. Of course not. There would be no need for that. Surely no lowly employee would dare to intrude upon the great man's privacy.

Great man in the son of a bitch's own mind, Longarm was sure.

Regardless, the door opened to a simple turn of the knob, and Longarm was inside.

A hat tree beside the front door held an assortment of light coats—necessary on these chill Colorado evenings—and, not surprisingly, a pair of gun belts.

One of those was probably Crocker's although Longarm suspected that would be worn more for intimidation than for actual menace. The other was Longarm's own trusted Colt, complete with belt and the holster that contained his badge.

He strapped the gun on. His hand was still cramping from digging his way out of the jail pit so he pulled the holster further to his left, almost over his left hip. He was quite frankly not as good a shot nor as deft a draw with that hand, but his performance was better than merely serviceable at either.

And damn but it was good to feel the weight of that revolver again.

Moving as silently as he could, he crept through the sprawling administration building.

Most of the rooms in the building were taken up with matters relating to the mine. They were filled with desks and chairs and plain, utilitarian filing cabinets. Down a hallway to the left he discovered a frilly bedroom that he had to assume was Amanda's, then a very nicely appointed empty bedroom. Quarters for visiting investors? Probably. Beside that was a water closet. Indoors! Amazing. And finally there was Aldous Crocker's own lavishly appointed suite of rooms.

The hall door opened onto a sitting room with a settee, writing desk, and fireplace. A dressing room was off to the side. It contained no less than three large armoires. Longarm snorted in disgust at a man who would be so self-indulgent.

Finally he found the man's own bedroom.

Crocker slept in a huge bed with a canopy, surrounded by pillows and lying under a fluffy comforter. Best-quality goose down would be Longarm's guess considering the way Crocker so outrageously pampered himself.

Crocker, Longarm discovered, snored when he slept. Bastard also wore a sleep mask.

Time to wake up, shit-for-brains, Longarm mentally resolved.

He considered how he wanted to do this. Finally he drew the Colt and with his good left hand aimed it point-blank at Crocker's forehead.

Then, using his right, hand he slowly unbuttoned his fly and flopped his pecker out.

It was time, he thought, to take that immensely satisfying first piss of the day.

Chapter 61

Aldous Crocker came bolt upright in the bed, urine drenching his nightshirt and some of the bedding. He clawed at the sleep mask that covered his eyes. He succeeded in knocking it askew so that it dangled from one ear but at least he could see who and what was assaulting him.

"You cocksucker," the great man screamed. "I'll have you hung up and horsewhipped for this. To death. To the death, I tell you, damn you. To the death."

Longarm stood and grinned down at him. "Really figure you're gonna do such as that, eh?"

"Yes, I will, I . . ." Crocker stopped in the middle of his rant, apparently having noticed Longarm's big Colt for the first time. The man must have been really and truly pissed off to have missed seeing it before now.

"Wipe your face," Longarm said. "You have piss in your mustache an' on your lips. Truth t' tell, that disgusts me. Pull your sheet up an' wipe off before I puke on you, too."

"What? I . . . Damn you!"

"Yeah, y'know something? People are tellin' me that all the damn time. I'm getting' a little tired of it. Now wipe your face."

Crocker turned away from Longarm and used a corner

of a fine, poplin sheet to scrub the urine off his face and out of his mustache.

But when he turned back again he was sneering. "Now who has the upper hand?" he snarled.

Crocker had a small, nickel-plated revolver in his hand. It was cocked and pointed at Longarm's belly. "Now you'll dance to my tune, mister."

"It's marshal, not mister, an' I don't see no need to dance." Longarm squeezed the trigger of his double-action Colt.

The .45 slug made a quite modest hole going into Crocker's forehead but it blew half the back of his head off coming out again.

"I sure as hell am glad I ain't the one has t' clean up this mess," Longarm said, looking at the moist red–and-gray carnage his bullet created. He looked down at his vest and with a grimace flicked away a pink gob of Aldous Crocker's brains, then carefully wiped his hands on the cream-colored satin coverlet over the dead man's bed before he turned away.

The next order of business, he thought, would be to look up Mr. Dolan. Perhaps, he thought with a chuckle, Dolan would invite him to breakfast.

Chapter 62

Custis Long leaned forward, picked up the whiskey bottle, and asked, "D'you mind, Boss?"

"Help yourself," U.S. Marshal Billy Vail offered with a wave of his hand.

"Care for some y'self, Boss?"

Vail shook his head so Longarm poured his own tumbler half full. Bourbon was not his favorite tipple but it sure as hell beat staying dry, and Billy just never stocked Longarm's preferred Maryland rye whiskey.

Longarm took a long swallow and shuddered. Damn bourbon was starting to grow on him. And it did warm a man's belly.

"I heard back from the sheriff down in Trinidad," Vail said. "The Chinese were all at Crocker's mine, sitting there waiting to be rounded up. The guards, of course, were long gone. So were their employment records so we don' even have their names."

"No harm done," Longarm said. "The men in charge were Crocker an' Dolan. Crocker is dead an' Dolan is sitting in the Denver County lockup waiting for trial. No, them I know about, but what will happen to the Chinese? They aren't supposed t' be here."

"And they won't be, not for very much longer. They will be brought north to the Union Pacific tracks and shipped on to San Francisco. From there they'll be put aboard a ship and sent home to China." Vail took a small sip of his bourbon, then said, "They were promised good wages. None of them ever saw a cent."

"D'you have the names of the other outfits that was s'posed to buy them as slaves?"

Billy smiled. "That we do. We'll pass out warrants as soon as a judge signs them. Then you and the other boys can go out and call on those gentlemen. And of course bring in any Chinese you happen to find. There are several other mines involved, a packing house, a heavy construction business. Pretty much anything that requires heavy labor and has a greedy cheat for an owner. I am . . . I don't know how to say this exactly, but . . . you far exceeded your orders, Longarm. You were not supposed to take any action. The attorney general was quite specific about that. But . . ."

"But?" Longarm repeated.

"But for once I am pleased that you bulled ahead where you should not have been. You did a good thing down there, Crocker's death notwithstanding."

"Let me ask you somethin' that's been worrying on me," Longarm said after a moment of silence.

"All right."

Longarm took a deep breath. "Damnit, Boss, why didn't nobody come when I sent that wire askin' for help?"

Billy became serious. "Custis, as far as we knew you were dead. And we never got the telegram you said you sent. I suppose the operator thought you were blowing smoke and he didn't want to use his time and the company's money for your bullshit."

"I may take a ride down there an' beat the shit outta that man, Boss. He sure put me through some grief."

"If you decide to do that, Long, let me know. I'll send another deputy along to arrest you afterward."

Longarm grunted. "It was a thought."

"Please leave it in the thinking stage," Billy said.

Longarm laughed. "Lordy, I'll never forget the look on Henry's face when I walked in that door, alive an' kicking. Your expression was pretty good, too, y'know."

Longarm tossed back the rest of his drink, leaned forward, and picked up the bottle again. "D'you mind?"

Billy Vail merely smiled.

Watch for

LONGARM AND THE SANTIAGO PISTOLEERS

the 381st novel in the exciting LONGARM
series from Jove

Coming in August!

GIANT-SIZED ADVENTURE FROM
AVENGING ANGEL LONGARM.

BY TABOR EVANS

2006 Giant Edition:

**LONGARM AND THE
OUTLAW EMPRESS**

2007 Giant Edition:

**LONGARM AND THE
GOLDEN EAGLE SHOOT-OUT**

2008 Giant Edition:

**LONGARM AND THE
VALLEY OF SKULLS**

2009 Giant Edition:

**LONGARM AND THE
LONE STAR TRACKDOWN**

penguin.com/actionwesterns

M456AS0409